A Voodoo and Vampire Mystery
A Witch's Cove Whodunit
Book 1

www.velladay.com

velladayauthor@gmail.com

Cover Art by Jaycee DeLorenzo

Edited by Rebecca Cartee

Published in the United States of America

E-book ISBN: 978-1-951430-48-1

Print book ISBN: 978-1-951430-49-8

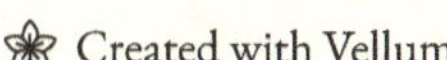

about the book

A witch, the granddaughter of a voodoo priestess, and a vampire walk into a bar. Only kidding. They are on a cruise to Mexico, but that's not the important part. What is important, is that when someone is murdered, the cruise turns into a ghostly whodunit.

Hi, I'm Rihanna Samuels, a 19-year old mind reader from Witch's Cove, Florida. Not to brag, but I received my first photo gig aboard a 55-passenger yacht for Valentine's week to Mexico! Can you say excited?

Everything is perfect, until I meet my roommate—some super rich, tattooed girl from New Orleans who seems to hate life. Yay, me. Believe it or not, things go from bad to worse when I find a dead body in our cabin. And that is only the beginning of the strange events that unfold. I'd give you a hint, but I don't want to spoil it.

Who the murderer is, I don't know, but solving a crime isn't new to me. Unfortunately, this isn't an ordinary case. After all, the murderer is still on board. All I know is that I'm going to need a lot of help to figure out who did it. Wish me luck.

chapter **one**

I BURST through the door of the Pink Iguana Sleuths' office in Witch's Cove, Florida. Not only was it the company that my cousin, Glinda Goodall, ran, but I also happened to live in the back room. It's a long story, but the short of it was that I had an absent dad and a mom in rehab. You know, the usual stuff, but I was lucky that Glinda helped me out two years ago by letting me stay with her.

"You look happy." That small voice came from Iggy, Glinda's talking pink iguana, who was blocking my way. This nine-pound lizard was her familiar. And yes, she's a witch.

Before I ramble on, let me introduce myself. I'm Rihanna Samuels, a nineteen-year-old photography student attending the local community college. In contrast to my short, blonde cousin, I'm tall, fairly thin, and have long, straight black hair. I used to only wear black, but I've seen the light—sort of. Now I've added blue and a few other colors to my wardrobe.

"I am happy, Iggy."

Glinda came out of the makeshift kitchen area. "Hey. It sounds like you have good news."

"I do. Beside the fact that winter break starts tomorrow, I

have a job!" I stepped around Iggy, slung off my backpack, and dropped down onto the office sofa.

Iggy crawled onto the coffee table. "I'm listening."

He loved to be the center of attention. I waited for Glinda to park herself before I began. Where her fiancé, Jaxson Harrison, was, I didn't know. I had hoped to tell them all at once about my news.

"I have a photo gig aboard someone's private yacht, though from the description, it sounds more like a small cruise ship."

Glinda's eyes widened. "How did you swing that?"

"A few weeks ago, there was a job posting at school, and my professor thought I'd be perfect for it. I applied, and today I heard back that I had been accepted."

"That's fantastic. Will you be the only photographer?"

"I believe so. Apparently, the woman who has been doing these cruises in the past is pregnant and can't go."

Iggy moved closer. "Why didn't you tell me that you were going to leave me?"

I sighed. Hadn't I said I'd just found out? "Iggy, I'm not *leaving* you. It's a job to gain experience. Besides, I won't be gone long."

"I need details. When is this event, and how long is this cruise?" Glinda asked.

"It's a six-day cruise to Cozumel, Mexico. All I have to do is take pictures of the guests, and then the ship will send the best photos to the passengers' email accounts. Piece of cake. The coolest part is that they are supplying me with an underwater camera that I'll use when the guests are snorkeling."

I didn't scuba dive or else I could have taken pictures of those brave souls too.

"That is awesome. Does it pay?"

I shrugged. "A little, but it will look great on my resumé. Not to mention how fun it will be."

"I am so happy for you. When do you go?"

"I have to leave tomorrow for a one-day orientation, and then we embark out of Tampa the following day."

"That's convenient. We'll drive you so you don't have to leave your car at the port and pay for parking."

I had the best cousin. "I'd appreciate that."

"Can I go on the cruise with you?" Iggy asked. "I won't take up much space."

He probably was looking for bragging rights with his friends. "I would love nothing more, but Glinda would miss you terribly. Beside, do you really want to be on a boat for a week? What if you fall overboard?" Yes, I was making that up, but I doubted the owners would appreciate a lizard coming with me and possibly scaring the guests.

"I'd be careful. Maybe Hugo can come with me to make sure I stay safe."

Hugo was Iggy's best friend, who happened to be a gargoyle shifter with a ton of talents—teleporting and remaining invisible were just two of his abilities. He also didn't eat or sleep, which made him the perfect bodyguard. "I would feel a little uncomfortable with him in my cabin. I have a roommate."

That, too, was just an excuse. Hugo could spend the night on deck. After all, he had lived many years as a statue on top of our town's church.

"Bummer." Iggy dropped down onto his stomach.

"Do you know your roommate's name?" Glinda asked.

"The email said she's Bella Benoit from New Orleans."

Glinda wiggled her eyebrows. "Sounds French."

"It does."

"I'm thrilled for you, but I'll miss you."

I knew Glinda would say that. "I'll miss you too, but we can video chat. They said there is Internet on board."

"Perfect. How many passengers are on this yacht?"

"Fifty-five."

She whistled. "That's quite a big number."

"I've never been on a cruise, so I don't know how many is a lot. What I do know is that I am looking forward to visiting Mexico."

"I'm sure you'll have an incredible time."

I smiled. "Thanks."

The next morning, Glinda, Jaxson, and my buddy, Iggy, dropped me off at Channelside in Tampa where the yacht was docked. Once I said goodbye to them, my nerves flared, though I didn't know why. Being a witch, I could read minds, which should have kept me calm. Perhaps it was the fact I'd never been on a large boat before. I hoped I didn't get seasick.

I had called my mom and told her about my adventure. As usual, she was worried whenever I went anywhere. I couldn't blame her. Dad had been an undercover FBI agent, and his job had been so dangerous that he was eventually murdered. Just to clarify, my mom had told me he'd died when I was about three or so, but that wasn't true. Dad didn't die until last year, but I was lucky enough to have had the opportunity to meet him before he was slain.

Last night, I had called my boyfriend, Gavin Sanchez, who was currently attending college in the middle of the state to tell him about the cruise. While he said he was thrilled for me, I could hear the longing in his voice. He wanted to be sharing the experience with me, but becoming a doctor required his total focus on school. As much as I loved chatting with him, the call made me miss him terribly, which made me more determined than ever to make the most of this opportunity.

A sign pointed to where I needed to go. When I made it

through the maze of people boarding a larger cruise ship docked at the port, I spotted a woman at a table sitting next to a pile of boxes with a stack of folders in front of her. The tablecloth had the name of the yacht on it: The Seafarer.

"Hi, I'm Rihanna Samuels, photographer."

The woman smiled and then looked through some nametags and folders. "Welcome aboard. Here is the information packet that details the layout of the ship, the location of your crew cabin, as well as the time of the first orientation meeting." She leaned over, grabbed three shirts from the box and handed them to me. "Your uniform."

"Thanks." I loved how efficient they were. "I can't wait."

As I climbed on board, I had to work hard to keep my mouth from hanging open. The ship was amazing. Beautifully decorated tables, surrounded by plush lounge chairs topped with fancy pillows, took up much of the stern. People wearing the same blue shirts that I'd been given were moving about, looking as if they were on a very important mission.

Before I could scope out the yacht, I needed to find my cabin and unpack. After checking the deck layout, I learned I'd be staying two flights below the main deck.

When I pulled open the door to my home-away-from-home for the next week, I was a bit taken aback by the amount of luggage and clothes strewn all over the room. To be fair, the cabin was really, really small, and there didn't seem to be much room to store things. One set of bunk beds lined the outside wall with a small cubbyhole for storage at the end of each bed.

There was a bathroom, but after I glanced inside, I wondered if a person could even fit in there. The space for toiletries was limited to a one-foot shelf. As for the closet? There really wasn't one—just a two-foot long rod to hang clothes on and four drawers.

Bella Benoit had already claimed the bottom bunk, which

meant I'd be sleeping on the top. That wasn't my first choice, but I wasn't going to argue. I'd been the last to arrive.

Considering my height, sitting up in the bed might not even be an option, but at least I had a place to sleep.

What I found a bit disturbing was the voodoo doll on her pillow with a few pins sticking in it. I hoped it was a joke since she was from New Orleans. Not one to judge—or at least I hoped I wasn't one to judge—I decided to unpack and not worry about Bella and her odd interests.

I located an empty drawer and neatly placed my three work shirts and a few other items in there, and then I shoved my partially full suitcase under the bed. I would finish unpacking after I had the chance to explore the rest of the ship.

Just as I was about to leave, the door opened. Words escaped me at who walked in, and I am never at a loss for words. Mind you, I was into the Goth scene for years, but this girl was over the top Punk. And yes, I had been surly, angry, and basically not a nice person to be around at one time, so I understood the vibe pouring off her. But this lady, who was about my age, took anger to a new level, and I didn't need to be a mind reader to hear her unhappy thoughts.

Bella was half a foot shorter than me, had bright magenta and green hair, purple eyeshadow, and black lipstick, not to mention several facial piercings. That wasn't what surprised me the most, however. It was the body full of tattoos. To be honest, I didn't think a classy ship like this would hire someone who wasn't even remotely close to being mainstream.

Deciding I should be the one to make the first move, I held out my hand. "Hi, I'm Rihanna Samuels."

She didn't shake it. "Good for you."

Ouch. "I take it you don't want to be here?"

"A real brainiac I see," Bella shot back.

I couldn't remember meeting anyone this distasteful, but I wasn't going to give up trying to reach her. Her emotional pain level was off the charts.

"Why take a job on a cruise ship if you don't want to be here?"

She waved a box of what looked like brown hair dye. "Why? Because my dad, in his infinite wisdom, decided that I was a lazy, good-for-nothing, rich kid." She huffed out a laugh. "In truth, he isn't far off. He said that if I didn't take this job, he'd cut off my trust fund."

I almost laughed. "What a tragedy."

"Mock me if you will, but my life is not all the fun and games people think it is. Money doesn't buy you happiness."

I never thought it did. My mom and I lived paycheck to paycheck, because my father supposedly died and left her with nothing—or so she said. In truth, he left his family for his job, though he did send my mom money every month, She never spent it, however, for fear someone would learn where it came from.

Years later, I discovered my father never visited because he didn't want to put us in danger. I understand that now, but at the time, his faked death affected me terribly. Hence my sour attitude as a younger teen.

When he was eventually murdered—and yes, I helped solve that case—he left me with enough money to live a very nice life. Other than paying for school, however, I haven't touched any of it. So yes, I was well aware that money only provided for food and lodging, and that it did nothing when it came to making friends or finding love.

"I understand."

Her lip curled. "Sure you do."

She was going to be a hard nut to crack, that was for sure, but I was determined to find a way to reach her. I nodded to the box in her hand. "I take it the owner didn't like your unorthodox hair color?"

"You could say that."

"I suppose you could refuse to change."

She stilled. "And what? Be thrown in the brig for the week?"

Once more, I almost laughed, but I stopped in time. "I only glanced at the ship's layout, and I don't think there is a jail anywhere on the boat. Space is at a premium, as is apparent from the size of our cabin."

"Nope. All ships have a jail—or rather a holding cell. It's the law, and trust me, my dad was the first one to point that out. He is well aware that I hate to be something that I'm not. He rightfully figured I'd refuse to adhere to their rules, which was why he told me about the jail."

That was harsh. "Hair color won't define you." She'd be just as unpleasant and angry with purple and green hair as with brown hair. "What job do you have?"

"Kitchen girl. I was supposed to serve the guests—and I will in a pinch—but the chef took an instant dislike to me. Go figure."

The piercings might have been the clincher. "How did the other kitchen staff react to you? Or haven't you met them yet?" I didn't know how long she'd been on board.

"I only met Haley. She was a blah."

A blah? "She works in the kitchen, I take it?"

"No, she's our maid. Her boss told her she had to make sure we keep our *stateroom* neat and orderly. As if."

Wow. Before I left to explore the ship, I wanted to ask about the voodoo doll on her bed. "Did you buy that as a souvenir from New Orleans?"

"No, I use it to hurt people. My grandmother is a voodoo high priestess."

Once more, I wasn't sure what to say, but I refused to

react to her comment that was clearly meant to rile me. It had been a long time since I'd met anyone like her, but I was confident that her story was laced with tragedy. "I see." I nodded to her box of hair dye. "Good luck with that. I'm going to check out the rest of the ship."

"You do that."

With that bitter departing comment, I left. As soon as I was on another deck, I pulled out my phone to call Glinda. Sleeping above this person might cause me to have nightmares—assuming I could even sleep. Would she stick pins in her doll with the intent to harm me if I wasn't nice to her? I don't know. In truth, the call was partly to obtain more information on Bella.

Since we were still in port, cell service would be excellent.

"Rihanna, is everything okay?" Glinda asked. She was correct to assume I wouldn't have called so soon unless something had happened.

"Not really." I explained about my rather strange roommate, and how she came from money. "Is there any way Jaxson can look into Bella Benoit? She's my age."

"Of course. Are you afraid of her?"

That was a rather insightful comment. "Not afraid, exactly, but I am leery of her. I don't know much about voodoo, but she brought a voodoo doll with her. She said she had it in case she needed to hurt people."

"Oh, Rihanna. Maybe you should quit and come home."

I wasn't the giving up type. "No. I might see if I can switch to a different cabin, though."

"That's a good idea. Do you want me to ask Hugo or Genevieve to teleport over and keep you safe?"

That was a tempting option, but I wanted to be able to take care of myself. "Not at the moment."

"Okay, but let us know if you need help. As soon as we're

back at the office, I'll have Jaxson do his magic on the computer."

"Thanks." An announcement came over the intercom for all workers to report to the main deck. "I have to go. Work calls."

"Be careful."

"I will." Though what defense I had against voodoo, I had no idea.

chapter two

THE STAFF—OR rather the crew as they were called—consisted of about thirty people, not including the captain, his first mate, or the engineer. I wasn't sure who I was supposed to report to, so I waited on the deck with the rest of the workers for instructions.

Eventually, April Crenshaw, who I learned was the head of staff, came out. She went through a long list of things we needed to know, like how to treat guests, where the lifeboats were located, and what drills we'd be doing. She then grouped us according to our positions on board—from maids to kitchen help—to discuss the specifics of the job. I kept looking around for Bella, but she didn't show up. Go figure. Following rules didn't seem to be her thing. Of course, she could be dyeing her hair and didn't hear the all-call.

Finally, April came over to me. "I'm guessing you are our photographer?"

I smiled. "I am."

"Great. The key to a good trip experience is for you to take a lot of photos while remaining invisible."

I knew what she meant, but my mind immediately went to

all the people—including Iggy—who could cloak themselves and truly be invisible. "Not a problem."

"Super. The rest of the information is in this packet." She handed it to me.

"Can I ask you something?"

April nodded. "Sure."

"I'm rooming with Bella Benoit, who I'm pretty sure can't stand me, even though we just met. Actually, I don't think she likes anyone. Is there another cabin I could move into?"

I never, ever complained about my circumstances, but there was something off about her that made me ask.

"I am so sorry. This is not a big ship, and as such, there are no other cabins. Just try to do your best. I understand your concern, but those who've been with us for a while are given the best assignments."

"That makes sense." I would have stuck me with the new girl too.

"Please tell your roommate that missing a meeting is unacceptable."

"Sure. No problem." I just hoped Bella wouldn't stick those pins in her voodoo doll aimed at me for delivering the unpleasant news.

After introducing myself to several of the crew members, I headed back to the cabin. When I walked in, the shower was running, and I could only hope that Bella was doing what had been asked of her. She was already in trouble with the head lady, and I wouldn't be surprised if she hadn't upset a few other staff members.

Not wanting to listen to Bella's rant about how her rights had been violated for having to be someone she wasn't, I grabbed my camera and left. I wanted to take some photos of the ship before the passengers descended tomorrow.

Without a doubt, this yacht was stunning and quite opulent. I really enjoyed taking shots of some of the crew working, as well as showing off how incredible the boat was. The best part was that I was able to stay away from our cabin for the rest of the day and even managed to avoid seeing Bella running about.

At six, dinner was served in the crew's galley. While I thought we'd all have to pitch in with the preparation, because the space was limited, only two people were assigned the chore of cooking the first night. Fortunately, I wasn't one of them and neither was Bella, who—no surprise—showed up late.

My roommate slipped next to me on the bench, which was kind of odd. Here I thought she disliked me.

"Well, what do you think?" She fluffed her short brown hair, but her expression was one of disgust, not delight.

"To be honest, I liked the colored version better, but I can understand why a ship would want the staff to look rather mainstream." Thankfully, she'd removed her piercings, which might make her life on board go a little smoother.

"I guess."

When she turned to watch the two guys cook, I hoped that was the end of our conversation, and I was not disappointed. I was just happy that she hadn't brought her voodoo doll with her.

When I woke up the next morning, Bella wasn't in the cabin, and I had to assume she was being trained in the fine art of kitchen duties. I imagined the chef hadn't been happy that she hadn't shown up on time yesterday. Since I'd fallen asleep before she came to bed, I was spared another one of her complaint sessions.

The guests would be arriving shortly, so I pulled on my Seafarer shirt, gathered my camera gear, and headed out. I forgot to ask about breakfast, but I figured I could find a roll or something when I had the time.

When I arrived on deck, April was there with a clipboard in one hand and a pen in the other. She looked up when I approached. "Rihanna, good. You're here."

"Would you like me to snap a photo of each passenger as they step onto the boat?" The shots would not be spontaneous or particularly interesting though.

"Yes, but only so that we can scan their faces and then tag all of your photos. That way, we will be sending the photos to the right person."

"The whole process is quite high tech."

April smiled. "It is."

For the next two hours, I took the pictures of the fifty-five cabin occupants. Most were couples, but there were a few singles. If I had to guess, I'd say the average age was between fifty and sixty-five.

As soon as all were accounted for, the ship got under way, and I couldn't help but experience tingles racing up my spine. I'd never taken a cruise before, and I was really looking forward to it.

By three, I was quite hungry, so I headed down to our galley and found some fruit, bread, and fresh coffee. While it didn't compare to our local shops at home, it hit the spot. I then returned to the main deck to study the ebb and flow of the passengers. That knowledge would help me take the best pictures possible.

That evening, between six-thirty and nine, during the passengers' first dinner, I only snapped a few photos since people with their mouths full wasn't a good look. But I did find a few couples on the top deck after dinner who were admiring the stars. Because it was a bit chilly up there, I didn't stay long despite wearing a thin jacket, but the shots I took were quite romantic if I do say so myself.

It was close to ten by the time I returned to the cabin. I was ready to download my photos and do a bit of editing on the pictures I wanted to keep. Happy passengers meant my performance review should be good.

I also wanted to have a private video chat with my boyfriend. Hopefully, Bella would still be on kitchen duty or out and about. Unfortunately, when I entered the room, Bella was sitting on her bed doing something with her voodoo doll. As much as I wanted to ask if she was able to wield any power with that burlap mannequin, I kept quiet. I was afraid there would be censure in my voice, despite *me* being a witch.

Wanting to appear friendly, I asked how her day went.

"It stunk. That chef will be the death of me." She held up her hands. "I rinsed and stacked so many dishes, my nail polish started to chip." The black covered only half of her nails, but I couldn't recall what her manicure looked like when I first met her.

I would have thought she would have worn gloves, though she might be against conforming like that. "That had to be tough."

"Yeah, it was. Then Haley, our maid, stopped in."

I could only imagine her response to our messy cabin. "And?"

"She said if I didn't clean up my stuff that I'd be assigned to maid duty instead of to kitchen duty. If she thinks I'd clean a toilet, she could—"

"I get it."

"No, you don't. You have a cushy job."

I had to stand, squat, and maneuver around objects and people all day. Taking pictures wasn't a walk in the park, but I didn't want to debate that with Bella. "I'm going to shower and then see if I have any good shots."

"Hot water only lasts like five minutes," Bella warned.

"Good to know." I normally loved long showers, but I understood that water would be at a premium on a ship.

Once I cleaned up and changed into my pajamas, I climbed onto the top bunk. I waited for Bella to ask some questions or make some negative comments, but she didn't, which worked for me.

I considered delving into her thoughts—assuming she wouldn't block me—but that would be an invasion of privacy. In all honesty, I didn't need my witch powers to know what Bella was thinking.

Before I searched through the photos of the fifty-five passengers, I texted Gavin to let him know how the trip was progressing so far. Just as I was about to send Glinda a message about my day, I spotted an email from Jaxson regarding my request to learn more about my mysterious roommate. I wasn't sure what good it would do knowing her background, but it might make it easier to deal with her if I understood her better.

Jaxson described Bella as someone who came from a wealthy banking family. Apparently, her mother had been killed in an auto accident when Bella was five. While her dad was busy building his fortune, she was raised in large part by nannies and her maternal grandmother, Cassandra Maurel. The included blurry photo of the grandmother had a caption that said she was a high voodoo priestess. The fact they lived in New Orleans suggested it might be true.

As I read over the information, my heart broke for Bella. Between watching her reaction to authority and how her preferences seemed to have been ignored, it painted a picture of a lonely, sad person.

I pushed her tragic history aside and spent the next hour downloading and then looking through my photos to determine which ones to keep and which to toss. I had a full passenger list, but until the staff matched the names with their photos, it would be impossible to catalogue them. My job was to make certain to capture the image of each guest at least once if not two to three times.

Eventually, my eyes began to blur, so I stashed my computer at the end of my bed, turned off my light, and closed my eyes.

I swear my phone alarm went off five minutes later. In reality, it was seven thirty the next morning, which for me was quite late. I never slept in like that, but maybe the excitement and sea air had exhausted me.

I listened to see if Bella was up and about, but I heard nothing. Either she was already at work or she was a very sound sleeper. I rolled over and slid off the upper bunk. When my feet hit the cold floor, a small chill raced through me. I checked on Bella who was asleep with her back to me.

"Bella, time to get up." When she didn't move or moan, I figured she must have been as tired as I had been. "I'll use the bathroom first, but the cook will be mad if you're late." Or so I assumed.

I gathered my toiletries and uniform and then headed into the very tiny bathroom. I'd showered last night, so I just needed to wash up, brush my teeth, and dress.

When I came out, Bella hadn't moved. I debated leaving her there, but I didn't want her to be in any more hot water than she already was.

I shook her shoulder. "Bella, wake up."

When she didn't respond, I leaned over and immediately gasped. A syringe was sticking out of her neck, and her eyes were wide open. A normal nineteen-year-old might have gone into shock, passed out, or screamed at the sight of a dead person, but since my boyfriend's mother was the medical examiner in town, I was slightly more immune to the horrors of death than most. Not only that, my aunt and uncle ran the funeral home in town.

My first instinct was to take pictures of the crime scene before I notified the captain. And that was what I decided to do. I figured a few minutes here or there wouldn't make a difference to Bella.

I hadn't heard there was a lawman on board, and I bet no one had a camera as nice as mine to record the tragedy, so I reached into the cubbyhole behind my pillow and extracted my gear. Having it in my hand helped calm my racing heart and mind.

Like I'd seen our Witch's Cove sheriff do many times, I photographed the room and the body. I took a close up of the syringe in Bella's neck as well as the voodoo doll in her hand.

Did she sleep with that every night? It really didn't matter now. Once I took the photos and uploaded them to my cloud service, I left to inform the captain of the tragedy. Fingers crossed he didn't think I'd killed her.

chapter **three**

"YOU DIDN'T HEAR anyone enter into your cabin last night or this morning?" the captain asked me.

"No, but I'm a heavy sleeper."

"I see. What's your cabin number?"

"We're in 1-C."

He nodded. "I'll have someone take care of the body. Just go about your business as usual and tell no one—and I mean no one—about this."

Really? "What about the cook? He'll wonder where Bella is."

"I'll speak with him. You just take your pictures. And remember to smile."

Wow. That was rather harsh. He didn't even offer any words of sympathy. So what if Bella and I weren't the best of friends?

"I will, but can I ask if you have a morgue here?" I didn't see it in the floor plan.

"It's required by law. Don't worry about a thing. I'll have my security officer look into her death."

"I didn't know you have law enforcement on board." Now I was impressed.

"He's mostly the muscle in case some passengers are out of line, but Mr. Weber will get to the bottom of this." The captain nodded to the stern of the boat. "Go on now. Take good pictures."

I wanted to ask many more questions, but I was certain I wouldn't be given any answers. If my cousin had been here, she would have pummeled the poor man to death until he gave in and told her what she wanted to know.

As was always the case—at least in Witch's Cove—someone would know something about what happened. Most likely one of the maids would be the best source of gossip since they seemed to be everywhere. For now, I would do my job and worry about who killed Bella later.

For the next few hours, I busied myself taking photos and worked hard not to dwell on the dead girl in my room. When I was finished, I figured some gossip about Bella's death had to be floating around. I just needed to find it.

One thing about being on a boat, the killer was still on board. We hadn't docked or stopped since leaving port, which meant it would be unlikely that someone new could have boarded the boat from the sea and left again without anyone noticing.

When my stomach grumbled, I headed on down to the crew galley. While I wasn't planning to mention Bella's death, I found it hard to believe others wouldn't bring it up—assuming they were aware of her murder. If they asked about it, I had no problem telling them what I knew—which wasn't much. I figured that since they were the crew, they should be told that there was still danger on board.

When I entered the galley, only two people were seated: Haley Stephens, the maid who I'd met, and a young man I'd seen doing laundry, though I didn't know his name.

"There's a casserole in the fridge if you're hungry," Haley said.

"Thanks." I was more in the mood for fruit, but to be friendly, I took her suggestion and heated a plate of the tuna casserole in the microwave.

"I heard your roommate died," the young man said.

Yes! I spun around. "She did. It was terrible. I found her in her bed this morning."

"She wasn't a nice person, you know," Haley said.

Ouch. I could see I wasn't going to receive a lot of sympathy, but that was okay. I doubted anyone on board liked her, which was a shame. Truth was, Bella did it to herself. She pushed people away. The sad part was that by being on this cruise, she had the chance to start fresh, but she chose not to.

"I know, but the murderer still needs to be caught."

The young man's eyes widened. "She was murdered?"

The line of gossip wasn't as strong as I'd thought it would be. "Yes. She had a syringe stuck in her neck."

Haley gasped. "That's horrible. Are you sure Bella didn't do it to herself?"

As in suicide? I hadn't thought of that angle. "It's possible. If I knew what was in the syringe, it might make more sense." Or would it?

"I have a cousin who's diabetic. Too much insulin can kill a person, you know," Haley said.

I had heard that. "Would one vial of it cause death?" If Gavin had been here, he might have known.

Both of them shrugged. "Was Bella diabetic?" he asked.

"Not that I knew of, but not only didn't I know her for long, Bella wasn't the sharing type." I reached across the table. "Hi, I'm Rihanna Samuels."

"Matty Wardroch," he said. "Nice to meet you."

We spent the next few minutes talking about the fact that the ship had a morgue, as well as some kind of security officer.

"Lewis Weber. He's no better than a mall cop," Matty

said. "He couldn't identify a murderer if he watched the guy shoot the victim in the head."

Since Matty possessed a very open mind, I couldn't help but read his thoughts. It was clear he was just trying to be cute, not cruel.

"Good to know. You guys haven't mentioned this to any of the passengers, have you?"

It looked as if I'd punched them in the gut. "Are you kidding? If any of the passengers learned of a murder, we'd all lose our jobs, because there would be no cruises anymore," Haley said.

She was probably overreacting—or maybe not. I slung my camera around my neck. "Work calls. And be careful."

"Let us know if you find out anything," Matty said.

"You too."

I left and took another few hours' worth of photos before the passengers went in to dinner. The timing worked out well since I needed to change out my memory card. While I wasn't thrilled about returning to the scene of the crime, it was my room.

No yellow crime scene tape blocked my cabin entrance, which led me to suspect it was either because they didn't have any on board, or they feared someone might ask questions why it was there.

When I opened the door to my cabin, I came to a halt. "Are you kidding me?"

There didn't seem to be any evidence that Bella Benoit had ever existed, and to think, this was a crime scene. They had already removed the body, but had they taken photos and dusted for prints, along with all the other stuff that went along with processing a scene? I understood that broadcasting to the passengers that someone had died would be bad for business, but this looked like they were trying to cover up something—like a murder. Ugh.

Since it was close to six, I decided to wait until tomorrow to speak with the doctor on board—assuming there was one. I wanted to find out if they planned to perform an autopsy, though with a boat this size, I highly doubted they had the facilities.

The best thing to do was to grab something quick to eat, and then after the dinner hour take some casual pictures of people in the bar having fun. Tomorrow would be soon enough to ask questions—questions the captain told me not to ask.

Right now, all I could think of was what would Glinda do in this situation? She'd research, so that was what I needed to do. But first, I needed to grab a bite to eat and then take a few photos.

Once I returned to the room after my rather short photo session, I climbed onto the top bunk. While I had wanted the bottom berth at first, there was no way I would sleep where Bella had died—or rather had been murdered. I didn't buy the suicide angle. Bella would have done something more dramatic if she'd planned to kill herself.

I could only hope that her death had been the killer targeting her and not some random kill. Why? I didn't want to be next.

I grabbed my computer and turned it on. I had so many questions. First, and foremost was why weren't we turning around so we could ask the Tampa Police Department to investigate?

After an hour of searching, I found my answer. For starters, this yacht was registered in Panama, which meant that country had jurisdiction. I also learned that a lot of cruise ships waited until after the cruise had returned to port before investigating a crime. The reason? They didn't want to upset the passengers. Didn't anyone see the problem with this line of thinking? At the end of the cruise, the murderer would be long gone.

That being said, I suspected it was a crew member who had killed Bella since she hadn't interacted with a lot of the passengers. And I refused to believe her rich father had paid someone to kill his own daughter. She wasn't that bad.

After I finished researching what I could, I turned to the job I was hired for. Trying not to obsess over Bella's death, I sorted through my photos. I'd just closed my laptop and was about to turn off the light when something caught my eye—or rather my attention. It was Bella sitting at the end of my bed.

I blinked a few times. Whoa. I must be more tired than I thought. "You aren't real. Go away."

Fine, I said that to calm myself. Of course, no one was there. The fact this

apparition—or figment of my imagination—had a voodoo doll in her hand, kind of creeped me out, though.

"I am real. Or rather, I'm as real as a dead person can be." One side of her mouth slightly quirked upward. "I guess you can call me ghostly."

"Sure." Yes, I'd seen many ghosts in my life—okay, maybe not a ton, but quite a few. However, they usually showed up when we called upon them to appear—like when we conducted a séance. Come to think of it, there had been a time during Glinda's birthday party last year when a slew of ghosts showed up unannounced. That meant Bella appearing for no apparent reason was possible.

To test that theory, I lifted my leg and tried to touch her to see if I met with resistance. I didn't. In fact, my leg went right through her. What that proved I didn't know. She still could be in my mind, but somehow, I doubted it.

"Satisfied?" she asked.

I curled my leg under me. "Not really, but I suppose you could be a ghost."

"Didn't I just tell you that?"

Since she sounded as snarky as the living Bella, I decided to interact with her. "I'm surprised you're here. Didn't you want to crossover?"

"No."

"I can understand that, but why come back here instead of visiting your family in New Orleans?" Bella hated this boat.

She seemed to stare at me. "Ah, duh! I need to find out who killed me."

Part of me had hoped she'd have been able to identify her killer. "What do you know about the circumstances of your death?"

She leaned back, though she probably forgot that she wasn't solid. "I have to admit, I am impressed with how calm you are."

I wished she'd answered my question. "Why is that?"

"Having a voodoo high priestess for a grandmother, I've seen my share of strange occult happenings, but few people can even see ghosts."

"I'm a witch, though I'm quite aware that not all witches can see spirits." Lucky me! I was one of the few who could see Bella. Okay, that was mean, but this woman had not instilled in me a lot of love and affection for her.

"Whatever. You have to help me find who killed me," Bella demanded.

I understood her frustration. I'd be frustrated, too, but the way to win friends and influence people was not by making demands. "Why should I?"

That seemed to stop her in her tracks. Bella looked down. "Because I'm scared?"

My soul broke at the first honest thing she'd probably ever uttered. "Okay. Where do we start? Who didn't like you?"

She laughed. "No one liked me. I'm not a nice person."

"Let's start with that. Why are you so angry?"

"You some teen shrink or something?" The bad attitude had returned. Death hadn't softened her one bit.

I held up a finger. "Yelling at me or being sarcastic will end our relationship in a heartbeat."

"Sorry. I...uh...can probably name a few people who I might have purposefully upset."

"Why would you do that?"

"I was mad at my dad."

Finally, we were getting somewhere. "Because he didn't pay enough attention to you?"

Even though she was kind of translucent, her eyes seemed to widen. "How did you guess?"

"I was the same way."

"No way. You're so..."

"I'm so what?" This would be interesting.

"Straight? Mainstream? Kind?" Her voice elevated with each word.

Each of those terms had a different meaning. I'm sure my mother would find humor in it if she heard that description. I had to credit Glinda and the Witch's Cove family for helping me understand myself. Perhaps this lost soul needed someone to help her too.

I could hear Glinda's voice—and maybe Iggy's—in my head. They'd both be saying: tag, you're it. You help her.

Fine. No one else was around, so I guess I was the chosen one. "I'm focused, that's all."

She shrugged. "So, will you help me?"

"I'll try, but the captain told me not to tell the guests about your death."

"Why am I not surprised? I bet if one of my dad's banks had been robbed, he would have paid the victims to say nothing. Image is everything to rich people."

That was rather cynical. "I can understand that."

She looked under my bunk. "I see my body and my possessions are gone."

"I just learned that when I walked in. They have a morgue here, so I'm sure your body is being treated well."

"Whoopee. Ten bucks says they don't have an autopsy room to find out what killed me."

"You're probably right, but when they return to port, they'll find out what happened." Assuming they weren't required to send the body to Panama. I wished that Gavin's mom had been on board. She could have done some tests at least if she couldn't perform a full autopsy, since that would have required a real morgue.

"How are you going to figure out who murdered me? You did say your cousin was a private investigator, right?"

I said no such thing. In fact, I didn't remember mentioning Glinda or the Pink Iguana Sleuths. Chances were, her father had investigated me, though not very thoroughly. Glinda didn't have her private investigator license. If Mr. Benoit did check me out, it was because he didn't want his daughter to bunk with a troublemaker. That implied he cared —at least a little—for her. "Something like that."

"Then you know what to do." She smiled, which I think was the first time I'd see her do that.

"Kind of. Tell me your top three picks for who possibly murdered you."

She blew out a breath, though I doubt it had any effect on her body. It was just another habit. "Chef Godfrey, not that I blame him. I might have told him he ran a lame kitchen."

"Charming, though that doesn't sound like a great motive for murder." I pulled up a file on my computer. "I want to take notes."

"Good idea."

Was that a compliment? I jotted down the chef's name. "Who else?"

"That main lady in charge of us."

"April Crenshaw. Did you upset her too?"

Bella nodded. "Yeah. I think I was late to a few meetings, though I did dye my hair and take out my piercings like she'd asked."

I typed what she said. "Anyone else?"

"Haley, the maid. She didn't like me at all."

No need to ask why. "Do you have proof that any of these suspects harmed you? Like did they threaten you in any way?"

"No, but I can sense these things."

"Because your grandmother has powers or because of being a normal human?" I asked.

"A little of both, I suppose."

Intuition wasn't going to solve this crime. Even if it did, it wouldn't carry any weight in court. "Before I forget, are you diabetic?"

"No, why?"

"It was a hunch."

"Whatever. What's next?" she asked.

"I have no idea."

As if the air had been sucked out of the room, a man appeared next to our bed—make that a ghost of a man wearing a tux and a top hat. Maybe the most bizarre thing about him was the wooden stake protruding from his chest.

"I might be of some help, ladies," he said with an abnormal amount of cheer.

Neither of us said anything for a moment. "And who might you be?" I finally asked.

chapter **four**

"MY NAME IS LORENZO BAMBINI, III, heir—or rather I was supposed to be the heir—to the Bambini family's holdings in New Orleans, Louisiana." The tall, thin man bowed, looking quite dashing for a dead person.

"Hi, I think?" Bella said. "Why are you here?"

He smiled. "When I saw your name on the death registry, I had a reason to rise."

"You know who I am?"

"Indeed I do. You are Bella Benoit, the great, great granddaughter of Estelle DeMieux."

Bella's mouth dropped open. "That's true, but how do you know that?"

"We'll get to that in a moment," Lorenzo said.

His comment was rather mysterious. "What did you mean when you said you had a reason to rise?" I asked. "Was it because of Bella?"

He held up a rather see through hand. "Not initially. I apologize. My presence must be such a shock to you both. Before I explain everything, I have to say that I am a little surprised that Bella didn't recognized the Bambini name." He glanced to the ceiling. "Then again, my family fortune might have been lost by now."

"Not if it's the same Bambini family who owns most of the casinos in town. They're alive and very rich," Bella said.

He grinned. "I'm so happy our family line is thriving."

Something bugged me about all of this. "Let's get back to this rising thing. Where were you right before this resurrection occurred?"

"I imagine I should have given a better explanation. I do apologize. My excuse for the confusion is that I died in 1922. The way I word things might have changed since my death."

"You think? 1922 was a hundred years ago," Bella burst out.

"Thanks for the date clarification, though I already figured that out. You see, we are taught that every one hundred years, a coffin will open. In my case, when it did, it enabled me to explore the world—in my ghost form, of course. You can imagine how excited I was to do so."

"Is there a time limit on this new freedom?" I asked.

"Most likely, but since I've not been dead before, I'm not quite sure. I never was a great student." He sighed. "I imagine I will tire and want to rest."

"Dude, if I'd been freed from a coffin after one hundred years, I sure as he—heck wouldn't have come to this ocean bucket," Bella said.

"You misunderstand, my dear Bella. I came to see you. Our families have been tied together for the ages. When I learned of your death, I had to help find out who committed this tragedy against you." He once more waved a fairly see-through hand at her translucent form.

That was quite sweet of him to want to help considering the short time he had on this plane of existence. "Before we delve into this case, may I ask about that stake in your chest? It seems as if your death was rather painful." That was an obvious statement, but the idea of a stake had a lot of implications. I, however, didn't want to jump to any conclusions. I knew I should have asked about his connection to Bella's family, but this seemed more important.

He tapped the stake, but his hand went straight to his chest. How frustrating.

"Oh, that old thing?" He chuckled. "Yes, the stabbing was unfortunate. I can't be certain, but I believe my family ordered a hit on me."

"How horrible." Why did he seem so at ease with that fact?

"If someone killed you, why haven't you looked for the killer?" Bella asked.

"I honestly don't care. Dead is dead." He held up a hand. "I had an idea that they'd try something like that, but in truth, I was carousing at the casino and having too good of a time to worry about such things."

Lorenzo was quite the strange fellow. "How did they get the drop on you?" I asked.

"I can see now that it was rather careless on my part. I wanted to catch a breath of fresh air, so I stepped into the back alley behind one of our casinos. I was trying to find my lighter to grab a smoke when someone came out of the shadows, wearing some kind of hood and stabbed me."

"Back up a second. If you suspected there was a threat, did you at least tell the police about it?" I asked.

He chuckled. "Oh, sweet girl. You are too young to know what New Orleans was like back then, especially with prohibition in effect. The police had their hands full and honestly wanted nothing to do with my powerful family."

"Then why not hire a bodyguard?" If his family was that rich, I bet he could have afforded it.

Lorenzo lifted his chin. "The Bambinis ask for help? Absolutely not."

"Why not?" The man was bad at explaining things.

"For the most part, we live hundreds of years, though a few of my ancestors were given the gene of immortality. I, clearly, was not. That being said, having a bodyguard is a show of weakness, and I already had one mark against me, which is what I suspect caused my family to want to *'do me in'* in the first place."

"Did you kill someone or something?" Bella asked.

He tilted back his head and laughed so hard that I half expected his top hat to fall off. Of course, it didn't. He was a ghost, after all.

"Oh, no, no. I mean, I wish I could have, but you see, when I was close to a source of blood, I froze—like when an actor has stage fright—and my fangs refused to drop. I was the black sheep of the family. My parents didn't want a failure to take over the family business."

"They killed you because you had performance issues?" Bella asked.

Lorenzo sucked in a breath. "Yes, or rather not quite. I didn't have *that* kind of performance problems. Oh, no, no. I'll have you know I was a real ladies' man. All the women loved me. And they had such lovely necks too." He sighed again. "Only when it came time to drink their *nectar* did my teeth fail to elongate or sharpen."

I looked over at Bella whose her eyes were wide open. "Just to be clear, are you saying you're a vampire?" I asked.

"Most certainly. Is that a problem? I promise I won't try to suck your blood. I am dead, you know."

I wasn't worried about a ghost harming me. It was that I honestly thought vampires were total myths. Okay, I probably thought werewolves were too at one time, and I know for a fact that they are very real. "Glad to hear it."

Bella twisted toward Lorenzo. "What is this death registry you mentioned?"

"Oh, that. Every time someone dies, the grim reaper has to put their name in a book. When I heard about your demise, I just knew I had to help."

I realized that I couldn't read the mind of a dead person, but once more his explanation sounded a bit fishy. How could he have learned about her death if he was in his coffin, unless he found out about it after he arose? However, it was the other part of his comment that intrigued me more. "You're telling me there are grim reapers?"

He laughed. "No. I was pulling your leg. I wanted to see how gullible you were."

"Not cool, dead guy," Bella said. "So why me?"

"Like I said, the Bambinis and the Benoits go back a long way. We were the two most powerful families in all of New Orleans at one time. When my coffin opened, I heard a voice telling me that you needed help."

"Like a spirit guide?" And no, I wasn't all that certain they existed either, but at the moment I'd be foolish to dismiss anything having to do with the occult. Seemed as if I'd been wrong about a lot of things, and I needed to keep a more open mind.

"I don't know what it was—or rather who it was. This person, or voice, wasn't visible like a ghost. It was as if he implanted the information in my head."

"How did you know where to find me?" Bella asked.

"I just knew." He smiled.

"Did this disembodied voice tell you that I was on this particular ship and on Rihanna's bed?" Bella asked.

He tapped his temple, though the effect didn't translate all that well. "I'm here, aren't I?"

"Question," I said. "I've read quite a lot about vampires in books. It claims that if a vampire has a stake through his heart, and if this stake is then removed, that he will be undead—or rather alive again. Is there any truth to that?"

"Not in all cases, but I do believe that it might be in mine. Mind you, the stake has to be removed from my real body—not from my ghostly form."

The whole stake removal thing blew my mind. "You're telling me that in one hundred years, no one wanted to resurrect you?" He didn't seem to be that terrible of a person. On the contrary, Lorenzo appeared to be rather pleasant.

"Apparently not. Those who were around at the time of my death should still be alive, or at least I assume they are, though it is possible they met the same fate as me. As for who is running the business that I should be taking care of, I'm sure my younger brother, Alexander, has taken over. If that is the case, he would make certain that I stayed where he thought I belonged."

How was Lorenzo not bitter about his untimely death? I surely would have been.

"I know why I haven't crossed over, but why haven't you?" Bella asked.

"I don't know about granddaughters of voodoo priestesses, but vampires don't *cross over*, as you say."

"Why is that? Is it because you hope someone will pull the stake out of your chest?" she asked.

"I'm not sure. Like I said, this death and leaving the coffin thing is new to me."

"Would you really want to live in our time though—permanently?" Bella asked. "We have computers, fast cars, and no time for family anymore."

That was a telling comment, but I kept quiet.

"What are computers?" Lorenzo asked.

"See? If you can't use one, you'd be lost. I don't know if anyone could catch up on a hundred years of technology. And unless your family took you back as a charity case, you'd have no money."

His mouth opened. "I'll have you know that my bank

account is quite robust—unless Alexander helped himself to my funds. If that's the case, I don't know what I'll do then."

The poor man had no idea what the depression did to the United States or how much inflation we'd had in the last one hundred years. However, at the moment he didn't need money. He was dead. "Just to catch you up, money doesn't go as far as it did back in your day."

"I see." Lorenzo didn't sound convinced.

"If no one removes the stake from your chest while your body is still in the coffin, are you stuck in this unearthly plane forever?" Bella asked.

"I imagine so, though I've never met a dead vampire before."

Bella waved a hand. "That's all nice and good, but if you're here to help me, what can you do?"

Lorenzo lifted his hand to rub his jaw, but he lowered his arm when he failed to connect with his body. Poor man. "I'm not sure."

Great. Bella might know who she'd angered, but Lorenzo didn't know anything about her stay on the ship.

"Lorenzo, can you teleport, move things with your mind, or cast spells? We need to know what you're capable of." Since I didn't know that vampires even existed before I met him, I had no idea about their talents.

"I made it from New Orleans to the boat instantly. That should count for something."

Bella and I looked at each other and shrugged. "It's a start," I said. "How about moving things? And I'm including Bella in this discussion. We need to know the extent of both of your abilities to see if we have any hope of solving this mystery. Are you like an ordinary ghost, or does being a vampire or a voodoo person carry special talents?"

"I don't know," Lorenzo said. "I've only been a ghost for a few minutes."

"All the ghosts I've encountered find it very difficult to remain visible for any length of time. Bella, you've been here for a while. Are you super tired?"

She shrugged. "No. I feel fine. Have I wavered, flickered, or disappeared or something?"

"I don't think so. Then let's start with something simple. When both of you were alive, what were you able to do—magic wise? Lorenzo, let's start with you."

"Hmm. I was a great cook, but that's not magic, nor is the fact that I had excellent taste in fine clothes."

He wasn't getting the point. "No, it's not. Let me ask you this: could you move things with your mind?"

"Of course."

"That's good." How a ghost could do that I didn't know. "Bella, besides sticking pins in your voodoo doll and harming people, what could you do?"

"If I needed anything really big to happen, I'd ask for my grandmother's help. She was powerful enough to summon the dead who could do some really bad things."

"That sounds promising. Like what?"

"Using the power in her hands, she and her followers could push back a group of people. It was almost as if she wielded an imaginary fire hose." Bella smiled. "And then there was the time when she actually created a wall of fire. Yeah, that was cool."

Her childhood was more destructive than I first thought. "I'm guessing you couldn't do any of that, right?" I asked.

"No, but Gran said she might be able to teach me." Bella then seemed to shrink. "I guess it's too late now."

"Who said it is?" I honestly didn't know, but why heap more depressing news on her?

Lorenzo lifted his arm, I guess to speak. "Yes?" I asked.

"When I was alive, I could hypnotize my victims—I mean the lovely woman—to succumb to my charms. Only once I did, I failed to suck their blood." He dipped his head in apparent shame. "So you see Bella, you aren't the only one who wasn't successful."

Ouch. I'm not sure that was helpful, but Lorenzo's situation was a sad one. However, we didn't need to dwell on that aspect of his life at this moment. "If you were able to have the women do what you wanted, that's something."

"My family didn't see it that way."

"Let's see if you still have that power. Make Rihanna do something," Bella demanded.

I held up a hand. "This isn't about me."

"Maybe not," she said, "but we need to fully understand the difference between our former selves and who we are now."

I wasn't certain of her motive, but I suspected she wanted to see him fail so she wouldn't feel so bad about herself.

I faced Lorenzo. "Go for it."

chapter five

"CLOSE YOUR EYES," Lorenzo commanded.

I doubted he asked his dates to do that, but I obliged. "Now what?"

"Listen to my voice. I want you to relax. Know that no harm will come to you."

Bella let out a little shriek, jerking me to attention, causing me to open my eyes. "What's wrong?"

"Nothing's wrong. Did you just do that stupid thing to make Lorenzo believe he still had what it took?"

"I didn't do anything other than close my eyes."

They both looked at each other. "Stop goofing around. We don't have time for that," Bella said.

I had no idea what she was talking about. "What did I do? And I'll know if you lie. I can read minds." Just not the minds of dead people.

"Lorenzo made you place your palm on your forehead and stick out your tongue."

"I didn't do that." No way could I have been hypnotized in only a few seconds.

"It's true," Lorenzo said with a lot of pride.

Wow. I guess he still possessed that talent. "Not to burst

your bubble, but what if the person can't hear you?" After all, he was a ghost.

Lorenzo floated down to the floor and appeared to sit. "I'm useless then."

This pity party wouldn't help us solve Bella's murder. "No, you aren't. You can move through walls and see who might be on the other side. And if people can't see you, you can spy for us. Actually, both of you can," I said.

"Good point," Bella said.

I was glad my embarrassment was over with and that their self-pity seemed to have thankfully disappeared. "Any other talents I should be aware of?"

"I used to be incredibly strong. In fact, I could lift a cart or a horse with little effort," Lorenzo claimed with pride.

That could come in handy, but I doubt he had that ability anymore. To test him, I looked around the room. I wanted to find something I didn't mind if he dropped. "See the pillow on the bed beneath me. Can you lift it up?"

"Of course." I leaned over the edge of the bed to watch. When he went to grab it, his arms went right through the material. "Or perhaps not."

He sounded so disappointed. One step forward and two steps back. "That's okay. Any other abilities?"

"I could transform into different animals, my favorite being a butterfly."

I shivered. "I'll never look at them the same way again."

"Change now," Bella dared.

"I'll try." Lorenzo attempted to remove his top hat but failed. Not being solid was a real hindrance to doing things. "I'm not sure what to do exactly. In the past, I just used to think it, and it happened."

"Close your eyes and picture a butterfly." I had no idea if that would work, but it sounded logical.

He did as I asked, and a second later, a beautiful Monarch

butterfly flew around the cabin. Bella clapped—or it looked as if she was attempting to clap since she didn't make any noise. Her actions kind of surprised me. It seemed as if she didn't have much joy in her childhood.

The butterfly flew toward me and landed on my face. "Hold on. I think I can feel you, Lorenzo." I lifted my arm and pointed my finger. "Land on my finger."

He did. The slight tingling of his feet caught me off guard. He flew off and turned back to being his tall, dashing self. "It worked!" he announced with cheer.

"The best part was that I think you were solid, or kind of solid. A butterfly might be useful in that you can could listen in on conversations, and report back what you learned." He could do that in his ghost form too, but I wanted him to feel a sense of success. "How about turning into a rat or a cat? Something a bit bigger."

"I never ever was a rat, but I'll try a cat. No one pays attention to them."

Except on a ship. I didn't imagine they are allowed on the Seafarer. Most likely, if Lorenzo were a cat, he'd be safe since I bet no one could see him. Once a ghost, always a ghost?

One second Lorenzo was a man and the next a black cat. This time I clapped. "You did it."

"I want to see if I can pet him," Bella said as she slipped to the edge of the bed and then stopped. "I'm afraid I'll fall. My legs might not hold me."

I didn't think she quite understood the concept of being a ghost. "Just float to the ground."

"What if I can't?"

I'd never seen this insecure side of Bella before. Then again, she did just die. I jumped off the bed and stood about a foot away from her. "I'll catch you." As if I could.

"Okay. Here goes." As expected, she moved forward and just glided to the floor. "This is so cool. I'm weightless."

"You are. Now see if you can touch or pick up Lorenzo."

Bella floated over to him, but when she reached to pet him, her hand went straight through him. "Darn. He looks so real."

That might be the best part of this. He was still a ghost. I bent down to test whether I could touch him. When I put my hand where I believed he was, I felt a slight pressure on my palm. I then tried to pick him up, but I failed, too, though I thought I sensed some weight.

"Lorenzo, see if you can move the pillow on the bed. A cat is large enough to do something, and if you were super strong before, you might succeed."

Unlike Iggy, he didn't seem able to talk, but that was okay, he understood me. The cat didn't float up to the bed as I'd expected, but rather he crawled up the side of the bed. When he reached the pillow, he grabbed hold and tugged.

It moved—albeit two inches. Well, I'll be. "You did it. Performance issues, indeed."

Lorenzo crawled back to the ground and transformed once more into his human form. "I'm almost alive when I'm in my animal form."

"That is fantastic," I said. "I wonder if anyone else on the ship can see you."

"I have no idea."

"I have a thought." I pulled out my laptop and moved down to Bella's bed. "It's a little late, but let me call my cousin. She's a witch, and hopefully, she'll know what's going on." I pressed the camera on the video chat program—and then waited. Knowing Glinda, she'd take a moment to find her computer, or maybe she'd just use her phone.

"Hey, Rihanna." She smiled for a moment and then her brows pinched. "Something's wrong, isn't it?"

"Yes." Not much was right. I went through the whole ordeal about how I found my roommate's body this morning, but when I returned later in the day, not only had she been removed, but her possessions had been taken too. "The strangest part was that the bed was made. It was like they didn't want anyone to know there had been a crime."

Glinda sucked in a breath. "That's terrible. Is there a crime unit on board by any chance?"

"No. The boat's too small for that. All we have is some mall-type security guy who I've yet to meet. As strange as that sounds, here's the big news. Bella came back as a ghost and wants me to help solve her murder."

"What?"

I figured she'd be surprised. "There's more. There are actually two ghosts here, and I want you to meet them to make sure I'm not crazy. I need to know if you can see them too."

Just then Iggy crawled up next to Glinda. "Let me see."

I missed the little bugger. His need for the spotlight never seemed to diminish. "Hi, Iggy. Okay. Let me turn the laptop around."

I faced it toward my two new colleagues. "They look dead," Iggy said.

I placed the computer on the bed and then sat on the floor next to Bella. "They are dead, Iggy. Bella was murdered yesterday, and Lorenzo left this plane of existence a long time ago."

"Cool," Iggy said, though I wasn't sure what he found exciting about that fact.

Glinda leaned in closer. "I don't see anyone."

I hadn't expected that. "But you see ghosts."

"True, but remember that even though Iggy saw the ghost of Mr. Hightower's cat, I couldn't."

"Her name is Sassy," Iggy said, a bit disgusted at his host.

"I know her name." Glinda shook her head at him.

"I remember that too. Anyway, I'm glad Iggy confirmed I am not imagining things. After Bella was killed, I took pictures of the crime scene that I'd like to forward to you. Maybe you can coordinate with either Steve or Elissa to see if there is something that will give us a clue as to what happened."

Steve Rocker was the town's sheriff, and Elissa Sanchez was the medical examiner, as well as my boyfriend's mother.

"I'll be happy too. Where's the body now?"

"In the ship's morgue."

Bella huffed. "They probably just threw me overboard."

She was being dramatic. "I doubt that." I turned back to the screen. "We'll be docking in Mexico sometime tomorrow, so we have a lot of work to do between now and then."

"Do you think the killer will remain on the boat or go on shore and then stay in Mexico? Because if he leaves, then you'll know who did it," Glinda said.

That would be a bit troublesome for another reason. He might never be caught. "At the moment, I'm not sure what I believe or what I hope will happen."

"I'm sorry this wasn't the fabulous trip you'd dreamed of, but there will be other chances."

I chuckled. Leave it to Glinda to put a positive spin on it. "Let's hope. If Steve or Elissa identify something in the photos that will help, call me."

"I will."

I closed the laptop and then faced the ghosts. "I guess that settles it. Few people will be able to see you, which should be to our advantage."

"How did that lizard thing see me?" Lorenzo asked. "And how is it possible he can talk? When I am in my animal form, I can't communicate."

"That *lizard thing* is an iguana, and Iggy is Glinda's familiar." I gave a fairly short overview of familiars.

Bella floated upward. "I'm going to see if my body is in the morgue."

"Do you really want to do that? It will be creepy seeing your dead self," I said.

"I'm cool with it."

"How will you open the morgue drawer and then pull out the shelf?" I asked. "And that's assuming you can get into the locked morgue in the first place."

She looked over at Lorenzo. "You said you were powerful, right?"

"I was, but not anymore. You saw that I couldn't even lift a pillow, and a cat isn't tall enough to do much. Though at one point in time, I could kind of climb walls. I was very agile." He sighed. "I didn't appreciate my talents when I had them."

"I think most people can say that," I said.

"I know," Bella said. "Rihanna, you can help."

I held up my hands. "Oh, no. I will not break into the morgue. It's illegal for one thing, and secondly, I can't pick a lock. Can you?"

She dipped her head. "No."

Lorenzo smiled. "Entering the morgue won't be an issue —at least for me and Bella." He then floated through the cabin wall and immediately returned.

"I forgot you could do that, but how can you open the drawer to see Bella's body?"

Bella tilted her head. "Why don't I just move through the drawer like Lorenzo here did with the wall and check it out?"

I pictured her ghost body floating inside. "You do know you'll be only a few inches from yourself?"

"Don't worry. I'll leave right away. Lucky for me, I don't think I can smell anything."

I raised my eyebrows. "What are you two waiting for?"

One second they were in the room, and the next they were gone. I grabbed my laptop, climbed up onto my bed, and dropped back onto my pillow. While I was still a bit creeped out with this whole series of events, I took my free time to gather my thoughts.

I really wanted to call Gavin and tell him what happened, but knowing my boyfriend, he'd hop on a plane to Cancun and insist I fly home. If he didn't have school, I might have let him.

While I had some peace and quiet, I sent the crime scene photos to Glinda. I could have emailed them to Elissa and Steve directly, but I wasn't up for explaining everything again.

Surprisingly, it took my two compatriots about ten minutes to finish their mission and return.

"We're back," Bella announced, sounding rather relieved.

I leaned back as she hovered over me. "Can you move to the end of the bed?"

"Oh, yeah. Personal space issues. I get it."

I didn't have space issues. I just didn't like some translucent entity, capable of who knows what, being a foot from my face. "What took you so long?"

"Ah, duh. We had to find the morgue. That stupid thing was tucked near the engine room. It was loud in there and not all that pleasant."

"I'm sure the dead will never complain." I usually was polite, but sometimes certain people pushed my buttons.

"Whatever," Bella said.

"I trust your body was there?" I asked.

"It was. I looked kind of..."

"Dead?" I suggested.

"Yeah. That. Thankfully, it was pretty dark so I couldn't see all that much."

Lorenzo floated toward the ceiling, probably thinking it would be easier for me to talk with him in full view. "Now that we've established Bella wasn't tossed overboard, what's next?" he asked.

"Next, I plan to sleep."

"No!" he practically shouted.

"Why not? I'm not dead, though I might be if I don't go

to bed now." I stretched out and then rolled over with my back to them.

"You have to help Bella," he demanded. "I'm sorry for being so insistent, but it's important."

There was something he wasn't telling me. I rolled back around and propped myself up on my elbows. "Why is that?"

Lorenzo glanced at Bella. "I should have mentioned it sooner, but her grandmother's grandmother, Estelle DeMieux, and I were...shall we say, involved. Helping Bella would go a long way to repay her family for me abandoning Estelle."

Bella swiped a hand at him. "What? Are you saying we might be related?"

He shrugged. "I have no idea, but I do know that Estelle was the love of my life."

"Then why did you abandon her?" Bella asked.

chapter **six**

LORENZO SIGHED. "I wasn't good for Estelle, mostly because I never told her that I was a vampire."

"Seriously? That would be an issue, but how did you hide that fact?" I asked. "Or am I completely wrong in thinking that vampires can't survive in daylight."

I never believed in vampires, but I had watched a lot of television shows and movies about them.

Lorenzo laughed. "That rumor has been around forever. Mind you, there are certain kinds of vampires who cannot be in the sun. My family must have bred with humans along the way to make it okay for them."

Bella lifted her chin. "I bet my great, great, grandmother dumped you since you were such a playboy," Bella said.

"I will admit that I love women and doing so came with consequences. Estelle was better off without me." He sounded sad.

"This family reunion is all well and good, but we have a murderer to find. We'll be docking in Mexico tomorrow," I reminded them.

"You don't think this person will run off, do you?" Bella asked.

She'd heard Glinda suggest that. "I hope not."

"How about if Lorenzo checks out the chef, and I wander about the rest of the crew cabins to see what they're saying about me?" Bella suggested.

I shrugged. "Sure. It can't hurt, but do you really think the killer is going to talk about how he or she stole the syringe, snuck into our room, and stabbed you?"

Her ghostly image sank to the floor. "No."

I held up a finger. "Bella, how about if you check out the infirmary to see if there is any insulin? It might be useful to know if they carry it."

"What's insulin?" Lorenzo asked.

I explained its purpose. "I think it was first used about the time you died."

"I know what it is," Bella said.

"Good. Then lead the way," he said.

Once more, they disappeared. So much for Lorenzo checking out the chef.

I dropped back onto my pillow and tried to think what our next move should be. Before I had the chance to think, someone knocked on my door. Clearly, it wasn't one of my two tagalongs since they couldn't make a knocking sound. Even though it was rather late, I slipped off the bed and answered the door.

A pudgy man I'd not seen before stood before me. "Yes?"

"I'd like to speak with you about the incident this morning."

Incident? Why did everyone around here act as if Bella's death was not very important. Furthermore, why didn't he find me earlier. It was late. "And you are?"

He wiped his right hand down his pants and then held it out. "Lewis Weber. You can think of me as the police around here."

Ah, yes, the mall cop. Matty described him well. "Sure, come in."

I was surprised when he looked around. "Which bunk was she on?"

Seriously? I thought he would have been the one to study the crime scene.

"The bottom one."

"When did you find her?"

"Around seven thirty this morning." The captain should have relayed what I told him. I explained how I spoke to her, but she didn't rouse. "I used the bathroom and when I came out, I shook her shoulder. That's when I noticed the syringe in her neck."

"Just one?" He jotted that down.

"Yes, one." Apparently, that was all that was needed. "I have photos of the position of her body and other stuff if you want to see them."

I could have told him to jump overboard, and he would have been less surprised—or angry. "You had no right to do that."

That was telling. "I was hired to be the ship's photographer."

"I want you to destroy those pictures."

That was just plain sick. "It won't do you any good. I already uploaded them to the cloud." And sent them to the sheriff and medical examiner of Witch's Cove—via my cousin, of course.

His face paled. "Have you told anyone?"

I didn't want to get anyone in trouble. "I told the captain." That wasn't a lie. I did tell him.

"Good. Do you have a theory as to who might have wanted to harm Ms. Benoit?"

Harming and killing were quite different things. "No. I'd only just met her during orientation. She worked in the kitchen while I was on deck taking pictures of the ship and the passengers."

He scribbled something else in his notepad. "If you know what's good for you, you'll speak to no one about this."

That comment rubbed me the wrong way. It sounded a lot like a threat. "Do you think I'd walk up to a random passenger and ask if they'd heard that one of the crew members had been murdered?" I lifted my chin to indicate I'd found his comment insulting.

Speaking to the crew was another matter altogether. They deserved to be warned that a killer was on the loose.

"We can't be too careful." With that, he spun around and left.

I was a bit dumbfounded by what just happened. Mr. Weber had done an excellent job blocking me out of his mind, but whether he was aware of it or not, I didn't know.

Did he have a motive for shutting me out? Who knew? Perhaps he wanted to solve the murder himself so he could receive all the kudos from some local police force. Or he could have been paid to look the other way. I sincerely doubted he'd been hired to kill Bella, though if he had been, he wouldn't want me digging up any dirt on him.

I hoped Mr. Weber wasn't being inhospitable because he believed *I* was his number one suspect. Come on. I had requested a room change, which should imply that I didn't want to be in the same room with her. If I had wanted to kill her, I wouldn't have asked. Ugh.

No sooner had I climbed back onto my berth than Bella and Lorenzo appeared. I couldn't tell if they'd been successful or not in learning if any insulin or syringes were in the infirmary. Having the two ghosts be partially transparent made analyzing their expressions a bit challenging.

"So?" I asked.

"We went into the health center. A nurse was there, not

that it bothered me much since she couldn't see us," Bella said. "I looked for insulin, but I only found one vial. There could have been more, but I didn't know what would happen if I tried to fit inside the cabinet so I could read every label."

I was impressed the boat kept the infirmary staffed all day long. "Did you think you would knock something over if you had?"

"Maybe. Yeah."

I didn't think she was solid enough to tip anything over, but her mind might still possess that power to move things.

"How about sticking a pin in your voodoo doll and aiming it at the killer?" I grinned. "Would that work?"

"Funny, funny. Like I can move a pin?"

"Have Rihanna do it," Lorenzo offered.

I had been kidding. Even if I did it, would it have any effect? I wasn't a voodoo priestess, nor did I possess any talent in that department. "I could, but don't you need something of the killer's for the voodoo spell to work?"

My comment was based on having watched a few movies that included voodoo. I was a witch, after all.

"Yes," she said.

"Good to know. While you two were checking out the infirmary, I had a visitor," I announced.

"Who?" Lorenzo asked.

I told them about Lewis Weber and his desire to keep me out of the loop. "I'm not sure he'll even try to find out who killed you, Bella. I'm sorry."

"That's the story of my life."

"Look, it's late, and I need to sleep. If you two want to do some reconnaissance, go for it. If anyone knows anything, it might be the captain." I had no idea if that was true, but I wanted them to stay busy so I could be alone.

Bella looked over to Lorenzo. "You up for more snooping?"

"Does blood taste good?"

Oh, yuck.

"Good thing no one can hear you, or they would freak out," Bella said and then smiled.

"What does *freak out* mean?"

Poor Lorenzo. Having been in a coffin for one hundred years seriously affected his pop-culture references.

Bella explained the idiom of freaking out and then the two of them left. Normally, I would have put on my pajamas, but I didn't trust these two not to need something in the middle of night and wake me.

I slipped under the covers and turned off the lights, hoping for sleep. Knowing me, my mind would spin with possibilities all night long.

Thankfully, I was wrong. I did sleep. When my alarm went off the next morning, I looked around the room, but spotted no one—or rather neither ghostly apparition. "Are you guys here?"

For all I knew, they were in the room but decided to remain invisible to save energy. Because my interaction with the afterlife had been limited, I didn't understand ghosts very well. Perhaps that was due to the fact that most of those we spoke with had only recently died and were almost as clueless as we were about things. When no one answered, I concluded I was by myself.

Since we would be docking right after breakfast, I needed to get a move on. I washed up, grabbed my camera, and headed out. Today, I was going on the tour to the Chichén Itzá Pyramids, and I couldn't wait.

My job was to snap photos of the passengers seeing the

sights, but April told me that if I spotted any promotional shots that they could use in brochures, I should take them too. It was why I was snapping away that first day, trying to capture the yacht's elegance.

When I entered the lobby, many of the passengers were making their way off the ship. As much as I wanted to speak with the captain and Mr. Weber, the wannabe detective, about the progress in Bella's murder case, I had a job to do. I spotted April, and she waved me over.

"Good, you're here. Russ Tremaine, the tall man over there with the short-cropped red hair, is the tour leader."

"We've met." Briefly.

"Sit with him on the drive over, and he'll fill you in as to what he has planned."

"You got it."

I waited a few seconds to see if April would address what happened to Bella, but she didn't. I found it hard to believe the captain wouldn't have confided in the head of staff, though her silence might have been due to the fact so many people were within earshot.

I scoped out the passengers, wondering if any of them were the killer type. Yes, I knew that was ridiculous since killers didn't actually have a type, but it was possible someone who was acting strangely could have been the assassin.

I exited the boat behind the last passenger. As I stepped foot on Mexican soil, I smiled. I was now a world traveler!

I was about to follow the crowd heading to the bus when I spotted the captain speaking with a stylish man in his late forties. His khaki pants, white shirt open at the throat, and blue blazer screamed wealth. It also screamed someone who was trying hard to impress. It was hot here. Who wore a sport jacket in a resort town anyway?

I probably would have ignored him, except that I spotted Bella's distinctively colorful luggage next to the man, which meant he could be Mr. Benoit. I understood why he'd want to speak with the captain about his daughter's death, but he had to know he couldn't just take her body, right? Though I suppose with enough money, anything could be accomplished.

The captain shook the man's hand, turned around, and headed back to the ship. I checked out the line of people loading the bus. I estimated I had about three minutes to chat with the person I hoped was Bella's dad.

Could he have arranged to have his daughter killed? It was possible, but if he did, would he fly down here just for her luggage? Again, that was assuming he was who I thought he was.

As for the luggage, I couldn't imagine there being anything incriminating inside her gear. Then again, I didn't know her very well.

I looked around to see if perhaps Bella and Lorenzo were here, so she could have confirmed the man's identity, but I didn't spot them lurking around. Where were the ghosts when I needed them?

The mystery man was walking away. I had to make a decision. And fast. Since my need to solve this crime took over, I rushed after him. "Mr. Benoit?"

He stopped and turned around. When I caught up to him, he stood taller. "Yes?"

Score. He was Bella's dad. To be honest, I was a bit surprised he didn't recognize me considering the information Bella had on me. Most likely, he'd hired someone to do it.

"I'm Rihanna Samuels, Bella's roommate. I was the one who found your daughter."

He set down the suitcases, his cheeks sagging a bit. "Do you know what happened? No one will give me answers."

I looked behind me. Most of the passengers had boarded

the bus, and Russ was waving to me. "I have to do a tour, but no, I don't know. Do you have any idea?"

He blew out a breath. "I've been racking my brain. This will sound crazy, but a man by the name of Don Shephard asked to borrow a large sum of money from our bank, and I turned him down. Long story short, he threatened to harm my wife if I didn't loan him the money. Just so you know, he never mentioned Bella in his threat. Because I wanted her out of harms' way, I arranged to have her be a crew member on this cruise. I was stupid to have thought she'd be safe. I should have provided security for my daughter."

"You couldn't have known she wouldn't be safe in the middle of the ocean."

Bella had told me her father wanted her to have a job so she wouldn't be another entitled rich kid. Perhaps he said that so she'd go on the cruise. Telling her someone threatened the family might have scared her too much.

Since he spoke of having a wife, clearly, he'd remarried since Bella's mom had died years ago. All I could say was that if the man was faking the massive amount of grief rolling off of him, he should win an acting award. "Could Don Shephard be on the cruise?"

Mr. Benoit shook his head. "No, I've had my security team watch him, but that doesn't mean he didn't hire someone to harm—or rather kill—Bella to get back at me."

Just then, Russ came up to me. "Rhianna, I'm sorry to interrupt, but we have to go."

I nodded to Mr. Benoit. "I need to leave. I'm sorry for your loss."

Not knowing what else to say, I turned around, and left with Russ. My heart broke for the poor man. It was possible that someone desperate for money could have hired a hit man to kill Bella, but there were two issues with that line of thinking. One was if Mr. Shephard was so in need of money, could he have afforded a hit man? And secondly, why not just harm Mr. Benoit—security team or no security team?

Ugh. I didn't know how Glinda always managed to solve the murders in Witch's Cove. Her cases, as well as this one, had too many unknowns and not enough answers. I just had to have faith that some clue would show up.

chapter **seven**

"WHO WAS the man you were speaking with?" Russ asked once we were underway to the Mexican pyramids.

"That was Bella's dad."

"Bella, as in the father of your wild roommate?"

I didn't think *wild* described her very well. Lonely and abandoned would be a better description. Though from what I just witnessed, her dad seemed to have loved her. Too bad she hadn't been there to see his reaction to her death.

"Yes."

"Why was he here?"

"He wants answers."

"Answers to what?"

I found it hard to believe that Russ hadn't heard about Bella's murder. His position as tour director should have made him one of the captain's *chosen ones.*

I needed to answer him. Even though I had a certain ability to read a person's mind, I felt conflicted doing so. In this case though, I decided to try. I studied him for a moment. The problem was that Russ' mind was sending mixed signals. I had the sense he wasn't sure if he should say anything, so I decided to help him. "About her death."

He stiffened. "Shh. No one is supposed to know."

Aha! He was a member of the captain's inner circle. Good to know. That—or he killed Bella. His motive, however, eluded me. "I know. I was the one who found her."

"The captain told me."

I appreciated his honesty, though I might have been happier if he said he'd heard it being whispered about. The more gossip the better. "Do you have any theories?" I asked.

He pressed his lips together and shook his head. "Not here."

Did that mean he'd talk to me once we returned to the ship? If so, that worked for me. As far as me giving him information, I was hesitant. There could be something sinister lurking behind those dark sunglasses. Since I couldn't read his eye movements very well, I decided to keep quiet for now.

I relaxed back into my seat and studied what Mexico had to offer. I also tried to listen to the various conversations on the bus. So far, the passengers were only talking about the good food on the ship and their luxurious accommodations.

Eventually, I blocked out their chatter and focused on the scenery, which was lush and evoked a sense of peace.

What seemed like forever later, we arrived at the ancient site. Once we all made it off the bus, Russ gave his history lesson about the Mayans. As much as I was interested in the ancient civilization, I needed to step away from the group and take photos of them.

Fifteen minutes later, the lecture ended and the group was free to roam about. I snapped photos of the pyramid as I followed two women who were headed there. For two women who were advanced in age, they sure took a lot of selfies.

I stopped behind them and pretended to be studying the stair-stepped structure.

"Oh, Gladys, the girls will be so jealous," the bleached blonde said to the white-haired lady.

Gladys smiled. "More so than our adventure in New Orleans?"

I froze. New Orleans? Jaxson was always telling Glinda and me not to jump to conclusions, but I couldn't help it. Bella was from there, so naturally my ears perked up. But then I shook the conspiracy theory right out of my head. There was no way these two elderly ladies could have been paid by Don Shephard to kill Bella. I knew I was being biased in thinking a man stuck that needle in Bella's neck, but it was always possible I was wrong.

The ladies chatted about the amazing beignets they'd had in New Orleans, which caused my mouth to water. When there was no mention of voodoo or evil spells, I figured it was time to move on to another group of passengers.

Wanting to be thorough, I walked by as many people as possible. Eventually, I spotted a man, around forty-five, standing by himself. I remembered him from the first day, but I didn't think I'd run into him since then. It was possible he took his meals in his cabin. That, or I wasn't as observant as I thought I was.

I snapped a few shots of him from afar and then moved closer. He stiffened as I neared, but he didn't turn his head to address me. That meant I had to start the conversation.

"It's remarkable, isn't it?" Yes, I bet that had been said hundreds of times, but I needed to say something.

"I find it an architectural wonder and quite peaceful." Instead of turning toward me, he remained facing the stone structure. The question I had to ask myself was whether a hired assassin would use the words, *peaceful* and *architectural wonder*?

Just as I was about to ask another question, a monarch butterfly landed on my nose. I was about to brush it away when I smiled.

The unknown man turned toward me and then leaned

forward. He blinked a few times. "I must have had a few too many drinks last night."

"Why?" I held out my hand, and the butterfly flew to my palm. I barely felt his presence, implying this was Lorenzo.

"The butterfly turned almost transparent for a moment. If you'll excuse me." The man spun around and walked across the field.

Seconds later, the ghostly image of Bella showed up. "That man was creepy, wasn't he?" she asked.

Lorenzo changed from a butterfly to that of his dapper self. I had to assume he'd always be wearing his elegant outfit.

"He saw me," Lorenzo said.

"Yes, he did."

"What did he want?" Bella asked.

"He wanted to be left alone, which is probably why he was standing by himself. Most people go on cruises to meet people, but apparently, he is the exception."

I then explained that I'd run into Bella's father, and that he was very upset over her death.

"Really? Are you sure it was my father and not someone working for him?"

Even in death, her pain was evident. "No, it was your dad. He wanted answers. Your father was grieving."

"Oh." Bella's brows pinched together. "What did you tell him?"

"What could I tell him? It's what he said to me that was very interesting." Some people came our way, and I had to turn my back. "Let's find a more secluded place to chat."

They floated over to an area devoid of tourists. With my camera at the ready, I sauntered over to where my cohorts were located, taking a few pictures along the way.

Once shielded by some stone edifice, I briefly told them about the possibility that a man might have wanted revenge against her father, which was why her dad wanted her to go on the cruise—to protect her.

She didn't say anything for a moment. "So it wasn't to make me have a job?"

I couldn't be positive, but it wouldn't do any good to speculate. "He said it was to keep you safe."

Her lips pressed together. "That was an epic fail. Did my dad say who this person was who might have killed me?"

"He told me the man's name, but your dad insists the man hasn't left New Orleans. If this guy is involved, it implies he hired someone to do the deed."

Bella floated about ten feet away and then returned. "We'll never find out who did this, will we?"

"We will. It just takes time."

"What about that man you were speaking with when Bella and I showed up?"

"It wasn't like I asked him if he killed Bella."

Lorenzo nodded. "I know you have a job to do, so proceed. In the meantime, Bella and I will put our heads together. When we return to the ship, we'll tell you what we learned, if anything."

I was about to say they better not be late returning to the boat, but then I realized distances probably weren't an issue for them—at least not for Lorenzo. Before I could ask them if they'd learned anything yet, they disappeared.

I inhaled and then remembered that I had been hired to take pictures of the passengers having fun. Yay, me.

Our pyramid time was up before I was ready, but I understood that a few of the people had an afternoon snorkeling adventure booked—and I was to take pictures of them. Snorkeling in the clear blue water would be wonderful.

The bus trip back was rather loud, because everyone was discussing the ancient pyramids. I tried to read some minds, but it was total chaos, so I leaned back my head and attempted to nap.

I must have dozed, because we returned quicker than I'd expected.

Once back at the docks, Russ took the microphone from the front of the bus and announced we had thirty minutes to change before the snorkeling adventure began. Everyone who had signed up was to meet at the base of the gangplank.

After he returned the mic to the driver, Russ stepped next to me. "Rihanna, I have your underwater camera for you. Stop by the tour desk, and I'll give it to you."

"Thanks."

When he didn't share his thoughts on Bella's demise, I hurried to my room to change into my swimwear. Hopefully, my two cohorts would be there to fill me in on how their morning went. When I pushed open my door, I saw no one. "Bella, Lorenzo?" I whispered.

When they didn't appear, I quickly changed. Tonight would be soon enough to find out what they'd discovered. Since it was highly doubtful I would find out anything about Bella's death while underwater, I pushed aside all of the questions I had about her murder and headed out.

Once I gathered my camera from Russ, I went down to the docks. The rather strange man I'd spoken to at the pyramids was there, which surprised me. He seemed to be such a loner—and rather sad. I figured one sightseeing adventure would have been enough for him.

Mr. Benoit's words came back to me about a potential hit man. Could this man be a hired assassin? One thing was for sure, I would stay close to a group while we snorkeled. I certainly wasn't going to become sidetracked and take pictures of pretty fish when a killer was on the loose.

Once we were all gathered, two guides gave us instructions on how to use our gear and then promised to point out the best place to swim to see the fish. After they passed out the life preserver belts, they loaded us onto a small craft and motored us out to a good snorkeling spot. For the next ninety minutes, I alternated between taking photos of the local sea life and the people enjoying themselves. I suspected this would be the highlight of the trip.

I tried to keep track of the taciturn man, but he seemed to disappear at will. Oh, wait. If he could see Lorenzo as a butterfly, that meant this man was a warlock, right? Or was Lorenzo actually visible to others when in his animal form? I should ask Lorenzo to change into a cat or a butterfly to see if Glinda could see him in that form. On the other hand, it was possible this passenger was like the two gargoyle shifters back in Witch's Cove who could teleport and become invisible.

My pulse sped up when it occurred to me that the killer could have teleported to our room, killed Bella, and then returned to where he came from. If that were the case, we'd never identify him. Stop it. Such negative thoughts wouldn't be helpful.

When our snorkeling time was up, I was relieved that no one else had been harmed. We motored back to shore and then returned to the ship. Once on the ship, I quickly made my way down to the lower deck to change.

Unless Bella and Lorenzo were still in sleuth mode, I was hoping to find them in the cabin, but that was not the case. Not wanting to waste my alone time, I rushed to the shower and cleaned up as quickly as I could. As I stepped out of the bathroom with a towel around me, guess who was there? Yup. Bella and Lorenzo.

"How was the snorkeling trip?" Bella asked, acting as if we were best friends, and she was interested in how my day went.

"Fun, but I didn't learn anything. No one is talking, and I'm beginning to think no one has been gossiping."

Bella smiled. "Maybe the passengers aren't talking, but the head of housekeeping, Roberta Strasser, was chatting up a storm while you were enjoying yourself."

This I wanted to hear. "I did have fun, but I was working. Let me dress, and then you can tell me everything."

I know that Lorenzo was a ghost, but I wasn't going to change in front of him, so I grabbed my clothes and ducked into the totally wet bathroom. Having the shower in the middle of the room was inconvenient, but I did the best I could.

After I attempted to run a brush through my long hair, I stepped back into the room. "What did you find out?"

"The captain asked Roberta to clean up our room so that there would be no evidence of my murder."

Darn. "That sounds rather sinister. Did she say if anyone took photos before she cleaned up?"

"They didn't take any—or at least not that Roberta mentioned. I have the feeling the captain has no interest in learning who the guilty party is. I think he'd rather let a killer go than chance the bad press."

I was afraid of that. "Who was she talking with?"

"That mall cop," Bella said.

"Lewis Weber."

"Yeah, him."

"I'd like to be a fly on the wall when Lewis and Captain Fenton are chatting. I have to believe your name would come up a lot," I said.

Lorenzo smiled. "I'll stay with the captain for a bit. In my day, the officers always knew things."

"Good idea. Check him out." I turned to Bella. "What's your plan for the day?"

"Depends on what you are going to do."

"I want to speak with the nurse or doctor. Some deadly substance was in the vial that killed you. Either that person stole the liquid from the infirmary, or he had the syringe when boarding the boat in Florida. The first event implies a last-minute murder, but the latter indicates premeditation."

"I agree," Bella said. "I'm thinking my dad might be right —that the man who couldn't get a loan was angry enough to kill me."

"I like that theory, but why go to the trouble of killing you? Why not harm or kill your stepmom like he threatened?" So what if he'd be hunted down?

She shook her head. "The house is surrounded by alarms and security. My dad is kind of paranoid. Killing me would be easier."

"I see." I tapped my chin. "That has me thinking. I should have asked your dad the date he turned down Mr. Shephard's loan."

"Why?"

"Think about it. If you're Mr. Shephard, you'd need a few days to come up with a plan to harm your father—or rather his family."

Bella smiled. "You're right. Hiring a hit man couldn't be easy. Then there is the fact he'd have to be able to book this cruise. I think my dad said that boats like these book up months in advance."

"When did he tell you to take the kitchen job?"

"He sprang it on me the day before orientation. I figured he didn't want to give me time to do something rash."

That was consistent with what Mr. Benoit told me. I mentally scratched her dad off the list of killers.

I dropped down onto Bella's bunk. "I'll speak with

someone who might know if there was any last-minute addition to the passenger list. Once I find that out, I'll check in with the medical staff. And you?"

Bella floated around, acting as if she was trying to think of something. "I'll stay around the infirmary. If something was stolen, they might try to buy more. They are in a port, after all."

I had to hand it to Bella. She was rather bright. "I like the way you think. Good luck."

"You too."

chapter eight

I WAS the first to admit that perhaps I'd misjudged Bella. That, or death had had a profound effect on her.

As soon as Bella floated through the wall, I quickly downloaded my underwater shots. Once I finished, I grabbed my camera, and the camera Russ lent me, and left to find out what I could about when had the last available cabin been booked.

I thought about asking the captain, but he might not know. Even if he did, he'd tell me to mind my own business. The last thing I needed was for him to hand me a ticket and tell me to fly home immediately.

Since this wasn't Haley and Matty's first cruise, they might know about such things, but I figured someone higher up would have more information. The only person I was even remotely friendly with was Russ. The best thing about him was that he knew about Bella's death.

I located him behind his desk in the main area. He must have been there to set up more shore excursions for tomorrow. "Hi, Russ."

"Rihanna. How can I help you?" He sounded very professional, which implied now wasn't the time to learn his theory as to who might have killed Bella. That was probably because there were quite a few passersby.

I handed him back the ship's underwater camera. "As I was sorting through the photos, my mind wandered. I know this many sound strange, but I was wondering how far in advance does this cruise book up?" My excuse for asking was totally bogus, but when he moved over to his computer, he must have believed me.

"We filled up in November. The Valentine's Day cruise is one of our more popular ones—as are the Christmas and New Year's Eve cruises."

That was a little disappointing. "The reason I ask is because there is this passenger who is a real loner. Why book a Valentine Day's cruise if you aren't into romance? I would think this particular trip would be booked by couples." True, there were a few singles, but they were elderly and might have lost a spouse.

"I don't know."

I refused to take that as an answer. "Is it possible, someone else booked the cruise and then found out they couldn't go, so they offered it to Mr. Loner Man?"

Russ faced me. It was as if he could see right through me. The tour director then leaned over. "Is this really about you know who and what happened to her?"

Ah, finally, he saw the light. "Yes."

He nodded to my camera. "Do you have a photo of Mr. Charming?"

"I do." I lifted my camera and scrolled through the pictures. I found a not so great shot of the man in question facing the pyramids. Then I remembered I took pictures of all the guests when they first arrived. I found that shot too. "Here is a better angle of him."

"That's Mr. Hackett." Russ typed into his computer and then smiled. "I remember now. You are right. A couple had signed up for both the Chichén Itzá tour and the snorkeling excursion. They contacted us a few days ago to cancel. I think the wife was in a car wreck. The next day, Mr. Hackett was assigned to their cabin. That's all I know. I don't deal with the reservations."

My mind spun. A car wreck? I really wanted to find out about that. While I didn't have the ability to hack into any kind of records, I wondered if Jaxson could do some computer research for me. "Where was this couple from?"

He jotted down the name of the couple and the town. "Don't tell anyone where you got this information. It could cost me my job, but I want criminals brought to justice. My dad was a cop."

Really? I liked that. While I'm sure some children of cops turned out bad, I'm betting more landed on the right side of the law. That was sort of like me, even though I didn't know much about my father until recently.

I folded the paper and stuffed it in my pants pocket. "I appreciate your help."

At some point, I wanted to ask him about his suspect list. I also wanted to follow up on what Bella told me about the missing syringes from the infirmary, but before I went in there, I needed to contact Glinda and Jaxson. The Internet service here would be better than on the open sea—or so I hoped.

My cabin was empty, so I climbed onto my bunk and turned on my computer. I always liked seeing the person I was speaking to, so I requested a video chat.

Glinda answered almost immediately. "Rihanna? Any news on who killed Bella?"

I loved how she shot straight to the point. "I'm not sure, but maybe." I told her about meeting Bella's dad who suggested his client might have had something to do with Bella's death. "While Mr. Shephard wasn't on board, Mr. Hackett—a rather strange man—may or may not be the hired gun. Here's the part that has my senses shooting to alert. The wife of the couple who had booked the cabin on this cruise was in a car wreck in Nebraska shortly before we got underway."

"Don't tell me that Mr. Hackett just happened to call that day to see if there was a vacancy?"

I did a mental fist pump. Glinda's mind worked the same way mine did. "I don't know the details, but it could have happened that way. That, or he was on a waiting list. That's why I was hoping Jaxson could find out more about that."

"Do you think this Mr. Hackett had something to do with the accident?" Glinda asked.

Iggy poked his head into view. "You see? You should have taken me with you. If Hugo had come, I bet we would have solved the case by now."

I had to laugh. I did miss the arrogant little bugger. "I imagine that's true, but I do have some help."

"Who? Those two ghosts?" Iggy shook his head, looking a little too human.

"What's wrong with ghosts? They are good snoops. No one can see them, and it doesn't take any effort for them to be in their ghostly form."

Iggy looked at me, which meant his eyes were focused to the side. "If you say so. If you need more brain power, let me know." After he basically told me off, he spun around and disappeared from view.

Glinda leaned forward. "He misses you. He's been like this ever since you left."

Aww. "I wish I had been able to have him with me, but it wasn't practical. But back to this case." I gave Glinda the information on the couple. "I'll send a picture of Mr. Hackett in case he shows up in Jaxson's search."

"We'll take a look, but like you said, it's possible, Mr.

Hackett was on their waiting list. He might have nothing to do with the couple or Bella's death."

"True. Russ never mentioned if the ship contacted Mr. Hackett or if it was the other way around." In the last few months, Glinda had developed this rather conservative attitude. I think she'd guessed wrong one too many times and was now trying to be more careful. "Let me know what you find out," I said.

"Will do, and stay safe."

I wish she hadn't said that. "I'll be fine."

Glinda tossed me a half smile. "Are you saying you think Bella and Lorenzo can save you from a killer?"

"Glinda! It's hard enough being in a confined space. I don't need you to add any more pressure."

"I'm sorry. Just lock your cabin door."

"I will." I thought we'd locked it the night before Bella was murdered, but maybe she'd stepped out to have something to eat and forgot to relock the door. When she returned, I'd have to remember to ask her.

Once we said goodbye, I stored my computer and headed to the infirmary. Inside I found two people—Bella and a nurse, whose name tag read Diana Uphold.

She smiled. "How can I help you?"

Bella was holding out her hands. "Tell her."

Thankfully, the nurse didn't respond to Bella's comment. "I was Bella Benoit's roommate before her untimely death."

The nurse glanced to the side. Because she didn't act surprised, she must have been aware of what happened. "I'm sorry."

"Thank you. It was tragic. When I found her, she had a syringe in her neck. Did you notice any missing syringes or any missing drugs?"

Her lips pressed together. "The captain told us not to say anything."

Why was I not surprised? "Right. He told me not to tell the passengers either. It would be bad for business, but I already know she died. I'm just trying to find out who killed Bella."

Diana hesitated. "Fine. Don't mention it to anyone, but we had a few things stolen on this trip. Thefts aboard a boat would do a lot of damage to our reputation."

Not as much as a murder would. "What was taken?"

"Some syringes and a few bottles of insulin."

This was excellent confirmation. No autopsy needed. "Would one shot of insulin kill a person?"

"If the person wasn't diabetic, absolutely."

"How could they get into the infirmary?" I didn't see any damage to the door handle or to the door.

"I don't know."

I had the sense she knew but wasn't going to tell me.

"How would they know where the insulin was stored? Had anyone come in requesting some and seen you open the case?"

She shook her head. "No. I wish I could help you, but that's all I know."

Once more, I doubted that. "Thank you." I looked over at Bella.

"I'll stay here for a bit to see if she tells anyone about you snooping around," my ghostly cohort said.

I nodded and left. Well, that was a waste. I hoped Bella, or Lorenzo, picked up on useful information.

Since I hadn't gone through my photos of our excursion to the pyramids or the snorkeling trip, I decided to do that now. Maybe something would pop out at me.

I was an hour into my work when I received an email from Jaxson. My hands actually shook as I opened it up. I read the details as quickly as I could, but it didn't reveal much. Lana Finley, the woman who had planned to be on this cruise, was driving at night when she ran off the road, hit a tree, and died. Jaxson stated that it was unclear from the article whether another car was involved or not.

"That stinks. That doesn't implicate Mr. Hackett, though he could be guilty," I mumbled to myself.

I wrote a quick note back to Jaxson to thank him. After I finished going through the photos and marking down how many people I'd taken pictures of today, I headed out again.

My main focus—besides taking photos of those who hadn't gone on either excursion—was to watch the passengers to see if anyone appeared to be angry at life. Why? I figured a serial killer wouldn't be a happy person. If Bella hadn't been the target, and a different person had died, she'd be on my suspect list for sure.

For the next two hours, I took pictures like I'd been asked, but my heart wasn't in it. I wanted to find something that would guide me toward Bella's killer, not provide happy memories for those on board.

When dinner time rolled around, I headed to the galley. Once more I was lucky in that it wasn't my turn to cook. If this hadn't been a private cruise, I bet they would have assigned a cook to us.

I sat next to Haley who was next to Matty. With the way Haley was leaning into him and looking at Matty with fondness, those two seemed to be an item.

Haley switched her attention to me. "Any news on you know who?"

I had lots of news, but I wasn't sure I wanted to share it with her, though I wasn't sure why.

Matty planted his elbows on the table, twisted toward us, and smiled. "If you girls are going to gossip, I want in on it."

I supposed I could use their eyes and ears. "Did you hear about the infirmary's break-in?"

"No," Haley said, "but I'm not surprised. The killer would have had to have located a syringe from somewhere."

"Unless he brought everything from home," Matty tossed in.

"I agree. You know what really surprises me, is how could someone enter my room if my door was locked—or the infirmary for that matter?" I shook my head. "I can't believe I didn't hear anyone come in."

Matty looked around, probably to see if anyone was listening. "It's not as hard as you think. Try opening the door with a credit card. These ships really weren't built for security. I've heard the larger cruise ships are better."

"Okay, that's a scary thought."

"Has Mr. Mall Cop questioned you yet?" Matty asked.

"Briefly, but I'm sure he will again. Since there was no evidence of a break-in, he probably suspects me."

"I doubt that. You didn't have a beef with Bella."

"No, but I asked for a room change. That should indicate I didn't like her much. But April said there were no other rooms."

Haley nodded. "That's true. We're full to the max."

"Personally, I'd check out the chef," Matty suggested.

"Why?" Sure, he didn't seem to like Bella, but enough to want to kill her? I'd have to remind Lorenzo that he'd promised to scope him out.

"She was rude to him and didn't respect his kitchen. Chef Godfrey doesn't like anyone to say anything bad about his food or the way he runs things," Matty said.

"Good to know." Thankfully, the kitchen crew was chatting away and making enough noise to drown us out. "What are your thoughts on Russ?"

"Russ Tremaine?" Haley shrugged. "He seems nice."

"Where is he from?" I wanted to know more about him. Not that I didn't believe his dad was a cop, but I wanted confirmation that Russ was a good guy. While I didn't read his mind, something flowed off him that didn't quite settle with me.

"I think he lives in Tampa now," Haley said.

Matty placed a hand on her arm. "Didn't he previously live in New Orleans?"

Needless to say, my senses shot to high alert. "When was that?"

He shrugged. "I never asked."

"Oh, yeah," Haley said. "I kind of remember him saying that his dad became ill last year, which was why he left New Orleans and moved to Tampa. He wanted to help out his mom."

"He mentioned his dad was a cop," I said. "Do they still live in Tampa?" They could have returned to New Orleans, assuming that's where they were from.

"I think so," Haley said. "I hadn't heard that either of them had passed. If he does live with them, it wouldn't be that uncommon. A lot of us live at home since we are on this ship for much of the time. It's not worth paying for two places."

That made sense. But Russ was in his forties, which made it a bit odd. "Thanks."

chapter nine

JUST AS I finished my conversation with Haley and Matty, many of the other crew members piled into the galley. Even though we made room for a lot of them at the table, a few decided to stand and eat. Two of those standing and chatting were Russ and April. It made sense they'd be friendly since both had prominent positions on the ship. And from the way they were whispering and leaning close to each other, they might be talking about Bella's death—or was it something more personal?

Because of the number of people at the table, I really couldn't mention my roommate's death again—or Russ Tremaine—mostly because I didn't need the captain confining me to my quarters due to my big mouth.

While I listened to the other conversations during the meal, I learned nothing of importance. Once done, I returned to my cabin and was actually happy to see Bella. I had a lot of questions for her.

"Hey," she said when I walked in.

I looked around. "Where's Lorenzo?"

"I don't know. He does his thing; I do mine."

I hope he remembered he was supposed to follow the chef

around as well as check out the captain. I climbed onto my bunk and dangled my feet over the edge. I had to lean forward a bit so my head didn't hit the ceiling. "Question for you. Did you know that the tour director, Russ Tremaine, used to live in New Orleans? That information came from Haley, by the way."

"No. Why should that matter?"

"Maybe your grandmother and he had a run in. I don't know. Could that happen?" I really needed to learn more about voodoo and what a priestess could do—other than call upon the dead and cast spells.

"I guess."

I waited for her to elaborate, but she didn't. "Are you able to visit and ask her?"

Bella stared at me and then blinked. "I don't know."

"I know you died here, so maybe your ghostly self just had to float from one side of the boat to the other, but Lorenzo is able to move around the world." While she had traveled from the boat to the pyramids, following someone might be easier than going it alone.

She snapped her fingers, but when they made no noise, she frowned. "I should try to find him. Maybe he can ask her! Are you thinking what I'm thinking?"

I didn't want to admit that I couldn't read a ghost's mind. "I don't know. Are you thinking your grandmother put a curse on one of Russ' relatives, and he wanted to get back at her by killing you?" I just made that up. I also doubted that was the case, but I needed to say something.

Her lips formed an *O*. "No. I hadn't thought of that, but it's possible. I've been known to put a curse on a few people too."

Why was I not surprised? "Would that person know that you put a spell—or rather a curse—on them?"

She planted her hands on the side of her face, acting as if I was asking a difficult question, but her palms went straight through her head. "Once more, you've stumped me."

"Here's a simpler question. Did you learn anything in your wanderings today?"

"Sort of. After you left the infirmary, the nurse spoke to the doctor about the theft, but I don't think they knew much. For the most part, they were concerned about the security on the boat."

"Oh, yeah, about that. Matty said it was easy to break into a room using a credit card."

"That explains things."

It might. "By any chance, did you go out during the night of your death for a snack or to get a breath of fresh air?"

Both hands raced to her mouth. "Whoops. I did. Do you think I forgot to lock the door when I came back?"

How would I know? "I hope you did, because if you didn't, it would widen our scope of potential killers."

"I'm sorry."

Nothing we could do about it now. "I will make sure to lock the door from now on." Not that anyone could harm Bella again.

She floated around the room from one side to the other, similar to our pacing. "Do you think someone is targeting crew members?" she asked.

"I hadn't considered that before, but I doubt it. There would be nothing to gain by it."

Lorenzo came in through the wall. "Phew. Spying takes energy."

"I imagine that merely being in your ghostly form requires some energy. Since you don't eat or sleep, it could put a toll on your body."

He smiled. "I think I've caught up in the sleep department."

I laughed. "You have." I quickly sobered. "Did you find out anything?"

"I followed Chef Godfrey around, but I didn't learn much, other than he is an unhappy person."

"Good to know. Did he happened to mention Bella's name?" I asked.

"In a way. He stated that he needed more help in the kitchen, and that he wished Bella were there, as bad as she was."

"Seriously?" she asked.

"Water under the bridge, Bella. We need to focus. Did either of you pick up any other clues?" They shook their heads. That stunk. "Lorenzo, you followed the captain for a while too. Anything there?"

"No, he just drove the boat. That's all."

I chuckled. "As a captain should."

"Maybe Lorenzo can ask my grandmother about those on the boat," Bella said.

Lorenzo pingponged his gaze between me and Bella. "Ask her what?"

I explained a possible theory that a person or that person's relative was injured because of a curse Bella's grandmother put on them. To get back at the voodoo priestess, they killed Bella. "It's a small possibility that Russ, who once lived in New Orleans, was the one affected by her curse. If so, he might be our killer."

"Good thinking. Bella, I know your great-great grandmother wouldn't put a death curse on anyone, since she was so sweet, but what about your grandmother?"

That was a good question.

Bella crossed her arms. "I'm not her keeper, but let's say I wouldn't be surprised."

I turned to Lorenzo. "Do you think you could find out?"

"*Moi*?"

"Yes, you. You know how to teleport, and Bella isn't sure she can. The last thing we need is for her to become lost somewhere in the hereafter and not be able to return."

Lorenzo floated over to Bella and hugged her—or at least he tried to wrap his arms around her. "We wouldn't want anything to happen to you, *ma chérie*. I'll go."

"Do you know where her shop is?" Bella asked.

"I'll find her. Trust me."

Before I could suggest he let Bella give him directions, Lorenzo was gone.

A second later, a knock sounded on my door, and I jumped a little, which wasn't good. It couldn't be Lorenzo. Hmm. Who would stop by now? Matty or Haley perhaps? Or was it Russ to finish the discussion about who he thought might have killed Bella? The only way to find out was to answer the door.

Without asking, Bella floated through the wall and a second later returned. "The mall cop is here. I bet he wants to question you some more about my death."

"Okay, but stay here. You can tell me things that I might need to know."

"Whatever."

That seemed to be her favorite expression, and here I thought death had mellowed her. Wrong again. I answered the door. "Mr. Weber. Come in."

When the portly gentleman stepped into the cabin, there wasn't much room for the two of us, let alone Bella. Thankfully, she retreated to my bunk.

"I don't like him," she said.

Oh, boy. I didn't need to hear her running commentary, but I couldn't voice my opinion. "How can I help you?"

"I've seen you whispering to some of the crew."

I stilled. "I have? What was I whispering about?"

"I don't know, but I'm thinking it wasn't anything good."

Whoa. He was a bully, and I wouldn't have it. When I was growing up, I was quite rebellious, which meant I could handle someone like him.

Come to think of it, I was a lot like Bella—angry and stubborn. "If you'd like, I can chat with you more often if you're feeling left out." I then flashed him a sweet smile—or should I have said a fake sweet smile. That wasn't nice, but some habits were hard to kick.

Mr. Weber pressed his lips together. "Since the harm has been done, I'll let it slide, but keep the topic of your roommate's death to yourself from now on."

"Really?" Bella asked. "How can you find out who killed me if you don't ask questions?"

I shook my head as subtly as possible. Good thing the security guy possessed no magic, or he'd have heard Bella.

"I hadn't planned to expand my gossip circle." Okay, I did want to speak with Mr. Hackett again, and maybe the chef, but that was all.

He cleared his throat. "Since you've been snooping, I might as well find out if you'd made any headway in learning who killed your roommate?"

Aha. So that was his motive in coming in here. "Me? The captain said not to discuss her case with anyone." He raised a brow. "Fine. As you've surmised, I've spoken to a few people —but not to any passengers. Unfortunately, I've learned nothing." I held up a finger. "That's not true."

I told him about speaking with Bella's dad, and the threat against him by the irate customer. That tidbit of information seemed to interest Mr. Weber.

"Does he know who this person is?"

I'd just explained that. "No, but it's possible this Mr. Shephard hired someone to harm Bella. Admittedly, killing is a bit extreme for not being granted a loan, in my opinion, but the loan could have been needed for a life or death situation."

Mr. Weber jotted down the information. "Anything else?"

"No, but I would like to bring closure to Bella—or rather to her father." Whoops.

"Here, here," she said, but I ignored her.

"I understand, but we can't afford for the passengers to learn of Bella's death. And please don't bother the nurse anymore or any other member of the crew for that matter." With that parting warning, he left.

So the nurse had tattled. Interesting. Did that mean she was involved somehow? There were too many questions and not enough answers.

I turned to Bella. "April asked me to take a few more shots from the top deck of the lights of Cancun. Watch my room."

"Why?" Bella asked.

I thought it was obvious. "I have been asking questions. At some point the killer might want to shut me up."

It looked as if Bella had sucked in a breath. "Don't worry. I won't let anyone come in."

Her comment sunk in. "Sorry. I keep forgetting that you can't really stop anyone."

Her shoulders slumped. "There is that. What do you want me to do then?" she asked.

"If anyone tries to break in, come find me. As I said, I'll be on the top deck." I would then contact Mr. Weber instead of trying to apprehend the person myself.

"Okay."

Once I reached the top deck, I made it a point to stand near a group of people as I took the shots of the colorful lights of Cancun. Not that I expected someone to come up behind me and do me harm, but I wanted to be extra cautious.

I was enjoying how the lights reflected off the water when someone leaned close. "Boo."

I jumped and spun around, my hand going straight to my chest. "Matty, that wasn't funny."

"Sorry, but you seemed to be in a trance."

"All the more reason not to scare me." Good thing I wore my camera strap around my neck, or it might have fallen overboard.

"Sorry."

"It's fine. What are you doing up here anyway?" Of course, he could go anywhere he liked.

"It's a beautiful night, and doing laundry can be a bit tedious."

I could see his point. I wouldn't want to be stuck washing the sheets and towels all day. Also, the small space allotted to the laundry room had to be warm, not to mention claustrophobic.

"Where's Haley?" I asked.

"I don't know." Matty actually sounded as if he didn't care, which was not the impression I had from earlier.

Footsteps sounded on the staircase. "Matty? There you are. I've been looking for you." That was Haley.

Matty turned around. "Come see the lights. They're really nice."

She wedged her way between us, probably to keep me away from her beau. I should assure her that I had a boyfriend and had no interest in Matty, but I didn't want to cause any more tension between them.

I lifted my camera. "I need to download these pics. Have a good night."

Those two lovebirds needed some alone time without me being there. Something must have happened recently, because I experienced a cold chill between them.

When I returned to the cabin, neither Bella nor Lorenzo were there. So much for her watching the cabin. I just hoped they weren't causing trouble—not that they really could.

I showered, crawled into bed, and downloaded my photos. I would have called Gavin, but he'd said he had a big exam coming up, and I didn't want to bother him. Knowing him, he'd sense something was bothering me. Considering I promised him that I'd never keep anything from him, he'd worry when I told him that a killer was on board the boat. Since Gavin hadn't called, I had to assume his medical examiner mom hadn't told him about Bella's death either.

While neither Bella nor her dad would have closure if the killer decided to head back home from Mexico, it might be for the best. Tomorrow, I'd hopefully find out if all of the passengers were accounted for.

After I worked on my photos, exhaustion overtook me. I stowed my laptop, clicked off my light, and went to sleep. I couldn't say what time it was, but a voice in my head told me to wake up.

I opened my eyes to blackness. Ugh.

"Rihanna, someone's in the room." I knew that voice. It belonged to Bella.

Someone was here? I hadn't heard anything. I sat up, hit my head, and grunted. Light from the hallway briefly filled the cabin and then the room door closed. My heart rate sky rocketed.

After a few tries, I managed to find the light over my bed and clicked it on. Bella was in the middle of the room.

"Are you okay?" she asked.

"You'll have to define okay. I'm not dead." I had managed to turn on the light, so I wasn't a ghost. "Who was in here?"

chapter **ten**

"IT WASN'T ME. I can't open or close a door," Bella whispered, though I wasn't sure why she was trying to be quiet. Few could see or hear her.

"I figured that. Could you see the person's face?" I kept my voice low in case someone was in the hallway.

"No, and it's not like I can see in the dark just because I'm dead, which really stinks."

"But you heard the door open, right?" I wanted to make sure I hadn't dreamt it.

"Yes."

"How about looking in the hallway?" Sheesh. I should have thought of that a minute ago.

Bella slipped through the wall and returned seconds later. "No one is out here."

"I knew I'd locked the door."

I slipped out of the bed onto rather shaky legs. I turned on the lights and checked the lock, but it didn't appear to have been tampered with. However, the lock was now in the open position, implying someone had come in. That knowledge gave me the chills.

"I know you said it was dark, but did you see this person try to do something to me?" If this person came into my room to harm me, what stopped him or her?

"Just that the person walked over to your bed. You coughed or groaned, and then he or she turned around and left."

That made no sense. I must have been in a dead sleep, because I didn't remember making a sound. Okay, when I sat up and hit my head, I'd grunted. "Why do you think a person would come in and then leave? Surely, a little moan wouldn't put him off. If he was the same person who killed you, he wouldn't have cold feet about killing again."

"I don't know."

Just then Lorenzo floated in. "Why are you two up? Or rather, Rihanna, why are you up?"

I told him about the intruder. "I'm not sure I can go back to sleep."

"Don't worry. Bella and I can take turns standing watch in the hallway if you like. If anyone tries to break into your room, we'll come in and warn you."

That would work. "I suppose if the killer is a warlock or witch, they will see you and not try anything."

"If you say so," Lorenzo said.

"Did you speak with my grandmother?" Bella asked.

"I did." Lorenzo shifted his gaze between us.

"And?" I asked.

"Bella's grandmother performed a few spells that were, shall we say, meant to harm, but she doesn't remember who requested the spell."

That wasn't helpful at all. I imagine she'd remember the recipient of the spell though. "Did you suggest any names to her?"

Lorenzo lifted his chin. "If I could have written down the

names of the passengers and the crew that would have helped, but even if you'd given me a list, it's not like I could have carried it with me."

Bella was still holding her voodoo doll, but she had it with her when she died. I guess that made a difference.

"I get that, but surely, you remembered the name of the chef and the captain?"

"I did. I told her about Captain Fenton."

I waited for him to tell me that Bella's grandmother knew nothing about him, but Lorenzo just stood there smiling. He must have something good to tell us. "What did Bella's grandmother say?"

"Some woman paid Bella's grandmother to put a spell on Captain Fenton's wife."

I pumped a fist. "That's great news. Why didn't you tell us this right away?"

"I like playing games."

I huffed out a breath. "Lorenzo. Bella was killed. This is serious. Play your games later."

He lowered his gaze. "You're mad, aren't you?"

I had no right to yell at him. He was just trying to help. If I complained too much, he might return to his casket, never to be seen again. "No. I'm frustrated and scared. Whoever came into the room upset me."

"I'm sorry, Rihanna. A gentleman should be more considerate. It won't happen again."

I was happy that he understood. "Thank you."

"Lorenzo, did my grandmother say anything else about the captain? I mean, if she put a spell on his wife, the captain might know we're related. He could have been the one to kill me."

"I didn't ask for details."

That was frustrating. "I'll contact someone who might be

able to find out about the captain's wife and whether anything bad happened to her as a result of the curse," I said. "I'll send a message now, but then I'm going to sleep. I'll be useless tomorrow if I don't rest. And thank you for volunteering to watch the door."

Lorenzo bowed and slipped through the wall to the corridor.

"I'll keep him company so you can sleep," Bella said.

That was very nice of her. "Thanks."

Once Bella left, I crawled back into bed, but I was too shaken to sleep right away. I pulled out my laptop and shot Jaxson a message. Normally, I'd be excited that we finally had a clue to Bella's death, but I wasn't sure this piece of information would pan out. I was hoping that Jaxson could do a background check on Michael Fenton to find out if he was indeed married, and if so, what happened to his wife. It was possible his wife had been harmed years ago. Without more details, I didn't want to draw any conclusions.

After I sent a message to Jaxson, explaining the best I could what I wanted to know, I stowed my laptop, turned off the light, and attempted to sleep. I didn't want to suggest that Genevieve or Hugo, our two gargoyle shifters, teleport here since they would have shown up in seconds, and I really needed to sleep.

I must have dozed off, because the next thing I knew, there was a lot of noise in the hallway. The sound wasn't directly in front of my door, but rather down the hallway.

Curious, I slipped off the bed, threw on my bathrobe, and eased open the door. If a killer was out there, one of the ghosts would have warned me. Come to think of it, why hadn't Bella or Lorenzo come inside and told me what was going on?

I peeked out. Really? The security guard, Lewis Weber, was putting cuffs on Matty Wardroch? Why? I reached out to tap Bella on the shoulder, but instantly realized my mistake.

"Psst." Both of them looked over at me, but thankfully, I didn't attract Lewis Weber's attention. He was too busy insisting that Matty needed to go with him somewhere. Since Matty was in cuffs, he didn't have a lot of options but to do what Mr. Weber asked.

While those two were arguing, I motioned for my two lookouts to return to the room. Not wanting Weber to see me, I stepped back into the cabin and waited for my snoops to enter. A second later, they floated through the wall.

"I can't believe Matty murdered me," Bella said.

"What? Lewis arrested Matty because he murdered you? What proof does he have?" I asked.

"He didn't say," Lorenzo chimed in. "He caught Matty trying to sneak into your room, and I guess he assumed the worst. We would have warned you, but Weber stopped Matty before he could get in."

"Sneaking into my room doesn't prove he killed Bella, but I'm not surprised Mr. Weber concluded that. The man's a bully. Do you think Matty was the one who came in a few hours earlier?" I shivered. Since he failed to harm me the first time, maybe he wanted to try again.

They both shrugged, or at least it appeared as if they were trying to lift their shoulders. Ghosts didn't exactly have muscles—and even if they did, I doubt they would be able to control them very well.

"It could have been him," Bella said.

"Did Mr. Weber state why he thought Matty was the killer?"

"No," Lorenzo said.

"Did he say he was arresting Matty for your murder or for trying to enter my room?" Things weren't making a lot of sense right now.

"For murdering me!"

"Bella, so that I understand, you specifically heard him say that?" Lorenzo hadn't.

"Not specifically. I just get the sense he did."

That wouldn't hold up in court. "How did Weber know Matty and I weren't...involved?" Of course, we weren't, but Lewis wouldn't know that.

Lorenzo lifted his chin. "I don't know."

"Then I need to find out. I can't believe Matty would have killed Bella. He's rather sweet."

"When I was alive, I watched enough crime shows to know that sometimes the guilty party is the person who is the least likely to have committed a crime," Bella said.

I'd used that reasoning many times in the past. "You're right."

"What are you waiting for?" Lorenzo asked.

"What do you mean?" I asked.

"Aren't you going to find out if your muscle man has proof that Matty killed Bella?"

"I want to ask him, but it's four in the morning. Tomorrow will be soon enough."

What sounded like a huff came out of Lorenzo. "Then let me see what I can find out." With that he floated through the wall.

I slipped off my robe and climbed into bed with Bella sitting at my feet. I really needed my sleep, but her determination to find out who'd harmed her seemed to take precedence.

"I still don't know why Matty killed me."

"We don't know for sure that he did." Though if he were guilty, I could think of a few reasons why someone would want to harm her. However, people usually didn't kill just because the person was annoying or rude. "Let me ask you this: did you talk to Matty a lot in the short time you were here?"

"How could I? Okay, well, maybe he did come on to me that first day, and I told him to take a hike, but that was all."

"Seriously? Why didn't you mention that before?" I asked.

"I didn't think it was important. I'm always telling people to bug off."

That was true. Anyone would have to know that Bella wasn't overly friendly. Then an idea struck. "By any chance, was Haley around when you did this?"

She looked off to the side. "Kind of."

"What do you mean, kind of?"

"Does it matter?"

Her bad attitude seemed to surface at the wrong time. "Maybe."

"Then yes. Matty kissed me, and Haley saw us."

"Matty kissed you?" Bella was terrible about giving details.

"That's what coming onto me means."

Not always. Ugh. Bella didn't seem to understand what information was considered important. "How did Haley react? I have the sense she is sweet on Matty."

"Who knows? I wasn't really watching her."

So much for an eye witness. "Full disclosure," I said. "Matty seemed overly friendly toward me tonight on deck. It's possible he stopped by to find out if he had a chance with me."

"You mean, date each other?" Bella asked, her face scrunched up in apparent disgust.

"Yes."

"How come you didn't tell him you were dating that college guy back home?"

"The topic never came up," I replied.

Just as I was about to turn off the light above my bed, Lorenzo returned. Had I not been intensely interested in what he had to report, I would have told him to tell me in a few hours.

"Well?" I asked.

"Apparently, these hallways have security cameras."

I sucked in a breath. "Then it showed who came into the room when Bella was murdered?"

"Yes, but the person was wearing some kind of outfit that blocked the face," he said.

"Like a hoodie?" Bella asked.

"I don't know what that is."

Bella described it rather well. "Was that what it was?"

"I believe so. Anyway, after Bella's murder, Mr. Weber was more diligent. He made sure to keep a watch on the cameras. I think he wanted to see if the killer would return to the scene of the crime."

"Anything else?"

"No, just what I told you."

I sank back against the pillow. "Why would Matty come to my room not once but twice? I told him and Haley that someone had cleaned up all evidence of the crime."

"I don't know," Lorenzo said. "I floated—if that is the correct word—into his cell, but he was alone. I tried questioning Matty, but he couldn't see or hear me. It is rather disconcerting to be ignored like that."

"I'm sure it is." Well, that was a bust.

Bella floated over to Lorenzo. "Let's see if we can find out anything. I bet that mall cop will want to fill the captain in on what happened. We need to spy."

Lorenzo partially bowed. "I am at your service."

As soon as they left, I dropped back onto my bed. After I turned off the light—finally—I tried to blank my mind to what happened, but I failed.

Eventually, I slept and awoke around seven. Even though I was dead tired, I managed to dress. Since the day would be spent at sea for our trip back to Tampa, there wouldn't be a lot of opportunities to take pictures, which freed me up to investigate. Most of the great shots had been the ones where the passengers were having fun in Mexico.

In case I was wrong, I slung my camera strap over my shoulder and headed to the galley. Maybe Haley had some information about what happened to Matty.

When I arrived in the kitchen area, four of the crew members were there, and Haley was one of them. She was chatting with Rosanna Sanchez, one of the maids. I grabbed a roll and container of jam from the counter, along with a cup of coffee, and sat at the end of the table, close enough to hear Haley's conversation, but not so close to appear to be eavesdropping.

While I had the ability to read a person's mind, that only worked when the person didn't hide his or her thoughts. Could I be certain what they were thinking? No, and that was the problem. Whatever I learned, I realized I could be wrong, though usually I wasn't.

"Rihanna?" That was Haley. I jerked my attention back to her. "I didn't see you come in. How are you?"

I wasn't sure why she asked. "I should be asking you how you are since Matty's been arrested."

Her eyes widened. "Shh. No one is supposed to know."

"It happened right in front of my door."

She huffed. "So I heard. I can't believe he was trying to sneak into your room."

"I heard the security cameras caught him. Do you know if he was planning to harm me?"

Her eyebrows rose. "You tell me."

What did that mean? "I don't know." It was why I asked.

"Are you sure you have no clue?" she asked.

Suddenly, Haley sounded rather accusatory. "Yes, I'm sure. I hardly know Matty."

"It didn't seem that way when I found you two on the deck last night."

Really? "I was taking pictures of the skyline when he showed up. That's all. I'm practically engaged to a guy at home."

That was a stretch, but I had a sense that someday Gavin and I would be together.

"Well, that's not what Matty told me."

Oh, boy. Jealousy was an ugly trait.

chapter eleven

"TRUST ME, if Matty told you that he liked me, it was very one-sided," I assured Haley.

Her shoulders sagged. "Oh. That's good to hear."

"If he and I were an item, would he really try to harm me?" Something was seriously out of whack with her logic.

"I guess not. Maybe he wanted to convince you that he was a great guy."

"That makes more sense. Matty doesn't seem like a killer."

"I didn't think so either, but Ted Bundy fooled people," Haley said.

Wow. That was a stretch. Here, I thought she had a crush on Matty. I guess I was mistaken. "Just so you know, in two days we'll never see each other again, but you two will. I don't plan on doing another photography gig onboard this ship again."

Haley's brows lifted. "Oh. Okay."

Phew. Now that we'd cleared the air, I wanted to address Matty's arrest. "Do you know why Mr. Weber arrested Matty?"

She leaned forward. "He thinks Matty killed Bella."

I pretended to laugh. "That's ridiculous."

"I know, right?"

Why didn't she act more distressed? "The security officer must have some evidence if he made the arrest."

Haley looked around for some reason. "A lot of people saw him kiss Bella that first day. She pushed him away and then laughed at him, acting like she was too good for him."

That more or less aligned with what Bella said. "Is that all? I mean, a lot of people are spurned by someone they like. I don't see that as a good motive for murder."

"If you're asking about fingerprints or him being in possession of any syringes, I don't know. I imagine Lewis has some hard evidence. But it's not like that mall cop would tell me anything."

"He is tight-lipped. Well, if you hear anything, let me know. I really would like some closure to this. I promised her dad I'd fill him in when we return to port." That was a lie, but it sounded good.

She smiled. "Sure."

I found it strange that she didn't ask me to help prove Matty was innocent. I guess she had little reason to think I could, even though she was aware I was trying to find Bella's killer—assuming Matty was innocent—so why hadn't she suggested we work together? Or, maybe Haley planned to be the amateur detective.

After I finished my coffee, I headed back to the room. Yes, I had my camera and should probably have found something to photograph, but I wanted to touch base with Glinda over this new development. Hopefully, she had contacted either our sheriff or our medical examiner about Bella's death. While I doubted Elissa, Witch's Cove M.E., would be able to shed light on what could have killed Bella, I needed to ask anyway.

Once in our cabin, I opened up my laptop and video conferenced Jaxson, since Glinda might not be up yet. She wasn't an early bird.

He answered right away. "This is a surprise." Jaxson studied me for a moment. "What's wrong?"

"Nothing's wrong. Not anymore." I explained about Matty trying to break into my room and then how he was arrested.

"That's good news, right? Or don't you think he killed Bella?"

"I'm not sure. There are too many holes. Did Glinda ever speak with Elissa or Steve about her death?"

"Yes, but all Steve could conclude was that from the angle of the syringe's entry, the killer was right-handed."

"That's good to know. Did Elissa chime in?"

He lifted his left shoulder. "She said she didn't have enough information to draw any conclusions, but one vial of insulin to a non-diabetic would kill the person. On the other hand, there are a lot of things that could kill someone."

"I figured." That was disappointing but expected.

Glinda poked her head into view. "Hey, there, stranger."

"You're up!" Good. I always appreciated Glinda's input.

"Surprisingly, I am. Iggy was restless." Just then, my favorite iguana showed his face.

"I guess you're calling to get my take on things," my pink little friend said.

I had to swallow a laugh. "Absolutely."

"Did you say that they arrested some guy on your boat for Bella's murder?" he asked.

Iggy had been listening. "Yes, but I'm not sure he did it."

"What did the accused say about it?" Iggy asked.

Iggy always impressed me with his large vocabulary. "I haven't been in to see him. Lorenzo, the ghost, went into the cell, but Matty couldn't see or hear him."

"I could go in," Iggy offered.

"Yes, you could, but Matty couldn't understand you

either, remember? Only witches, warlocks, or those who had a spell put on them can."

"Fine. Then what about Genevieve?"

Since Genevieve would appear human, Matty could see and hear her. And she could be here in seconds. "The only problem is that he'd freak out if a woman suddenly appeared in his cell."

"Rihanna," Glinda said. "I like the idea of her being there. If you don't think this Matty person is guilty, then the killer is still at large. How about if I tell her to appear outside of the cell?"

That could work. "But how can I tell her where I am—other than in the middle of the Gulf of Mexico?"

"You have your phone," Jaxson said. "It will have your coordinates. Maybe she can find you from that, though I can't say for sure."

Glinda held up a finger. "Let me ask her."

My cousin called Genevieve, who like my ghosts, didn't eat or sleep. The conversation was short. Why? With Genevieve, she had a tendency to act before thinking. A second later, she had teleported into Glinda and Jaxson's office.

"Hi," the gargoyle shifter said. "Glinda said you needed help?"

"Yes, but it's complicated." I explained about my roommate's death, though I suspected Iggy had already filled her in. "We need to find out from the accused what he was doing at my door, and if he killed Bella."

She smiled. "Don't you worry. We'll find that out. No problem."

"We?"

"It's better when Hugo is with me."

Hugo was her fellow gargoyle shifter—one who had many talents. Getting someone to tell the truth was just one of them. "Fine, but do you think you can find us in the middle of the Gulf? I have the coordinates."

"I hope so."

She didn't sound all that confident, but I gave her the information. "I'm on the bottom deck in cabin 1-C. Maybe you should come here first."

"Okay." Genevieve waved goodbye and then disappeared.

Glinda shrugged. "Good old Genevieve. Is there anything else we can help with?"

"Not at the moment. I'll be back in two days. I'm hoping all will be quiet until then."

"Hi!" That came from Genevieve who was standing, with Hugo, in the middle of my cabin.

"Glinda, Jaxson, and Iggy. I need to go. Genevieve and Hugo are here." Iggy spun around and crawled off the table. "Is he mad?" I asked.

"I think he wanted Genevieve to take him with her."

That sounded like Iggy. "Maybe next time."

I disconnected and faced my two other cohorts. "Thanks for coming."

"No problem," Genevieve said. "Where is the jail?"

"I don't know." Lorenzo knew, but neither he nor Bella were here. "How about if you two cloak yourselves and follow me? I'll find Mr. Weber—the man who arrested Matty. I'll ask if I can speak with Matty. He'll say no, but at least we might learn where he is being held."

"Sounds good."

We left together, or sort of together, since my shifter friends had cloaked themselves. I had my camera with me since I wanted people to think I was doing my job. Genevieve seemed to understand that chatting with me might not be good since someone might hear her and wonder where the voice was coming from.

I wasn't sure where to find Lewis Weber, but April might know. By chance, I found her near the galley.

"April. I'm glad I ran into you. I need to speak with Mr. Weber about something. Do you know where I can find him?"

"He's on the floor above us, near the stern. He has an office back there."

"Thanks." I should have spent more time exploring the ship, but the engine area hadn't held much appeal. Before she had the chance to ask why I needed to see him, I left.

It didn't take long for me to find his office. I knocked, hoping he was inside instead of making sure the ship was secure.

A chair leg scraped and then the door opened. "Rihanna," he growled.

The man was not a friendly person. "I was wondering if I could speak with Matty."

He straightened. "I'm afraid I can't allow that."

"Why not? I want to find out why he was trying to enter my room."

Mr. Weber shook his head. "It's against policy."

I doubted that. I looked around. "Where is he being held? I only ask so that I won't go near there."

"He's next door."

I backed away, pretending as if I was afraid Matty would burst out of the cell at any moment. "Okay, thanks."

With that I spun around and headed back to my cabin. I could only hope that Genevieve and Hugo could discover Matty's side of the story.

I was only in the room about ten minutes when Bella and Lorenzo showed up.

Bella looked around. "I sensed someone's been here. There's more energy than usual."

That was an interesting talent I didn't know she possessed.

Too bad I couldn't tell if she was angry or merely curious. "Yes. My friends came."

"Friends? Who? How did they get here?"

I explained about the gargoyle shifters.

"Why are they here?" she asked. I hadn't meant to upset her, but apparently, I had. I honestly thought Bella would be happy that we had reinforcements.

I told my ghostly friends about contacting Glinda, and how we thought someone who was alive and who had the ability to remain invisible could speak with Matty. "I'm expecting them to return shortly."

Before either of them could ask any other questions, Hugo and Genevieve appeared. That was good timing. I introduced them to each other. Genevieve, who was Ms. Congeniality, was very interested in Bella and her voodoo talents, which softened my roommate's attitude. As much as I enjoyed them bonding, I wanted to find out what Matty had to say.

I cleared my throat. "I hate to cut short the social hour, but did you and Hugo find out anything from Matty?"

"Yes," Genevieve said.

As usual, she didn't elaborate until I asked. "What did you find out?"

"Matty said he went to your cabin twice to make sure you were okay. The second time he never made it inside."

So he was the person who snuck in. "Why didn't he knock?"

"He didn't want to scare you. It was in the middle of the night after all."

That was considerate of him. "Why did he need to see if I was okay?"

She inhaled. "Hugo had to dig that information out from his mind, but apparently, Matty overheard some people talking about the fact that you needed to be silenced."

If I hadn't been surrounded by two very powerful people,

I might have been afraid. "What does that mean?" Okay, I could figure it out. "Do you mean kill me? Like they did to Bella?"

"Matty didn't hear everything, but he thinks so."

"If that is true, why not tell me to my face."

Genevieve looked over at Hugo and did her telepathic communication thing with him. She turned back to us. "I think he just found out about the threat."

"I don't understand why he ran away after he came inside. Why not tell me then?" I asked.

Genevieve shrugged. "Matty might have thought it best if he just watched over you. If you knew you might be in danger, you could have spoken to the wrong person."

"That's probably true. I might have confided my concern to the killer himself. Did Matty know who wanted to harm me or who killed Bella?"

"No."

Feeling a bit claustrophobic with so many people in the small cabin, I sat down on the bottom bunk next to Bella. "Do any of you have any suggestions what we should do next?"

"Yes," Genevieve said.

When she once more didn't continue, I dipped my chin.

"We need to remove you from the ship," she said.

I held up a hand. "You can't do that."

"Oh, yes, I can."

In a flash, she grabbed my shoulder, and I was instantly teleported back to Witch's Cove, Florida to Glinda and Jaxson's office—aka where I lived.

"Rihanna?" Glinda's eyes were understandably open wide.

I spun to face Genevieve. "You can't just whisk me away like that. People will miss me. And why am I here anyway?" I held up a hand. "It doesn't matter. You have to return me, right now."

"I just told you that Matty believes that you're in danger."

"Danger?" Glinda asked. "The young man who was arrested is innocent?"

"I think so, at least according to Hugo and Genevieve he is," I said.

Hugo suddenly appeared next to Genevieve. I don't know why he hadn't teleported with Genevieve, but perhaps he wanted to see if he could communicate with the ghosts. That would be interesting if he could, not that he'd ever see them again.

"Then you should stay here," Glinda said.

Iggy crawled over to me. Out of habit, I bent down and picked him up. "I've missed you, buddy."

"You wouldn't have had to miss me if you'd taken me with you."

I'd already explained how that wouldn't have worked. "I know."

Genevieve touched my shoulder again. For a moment, I thought she was going to teleport me back to the ship. "Hugo and I will figure this out."

"Figure what out? Who killed Bella or who wants to harm me?"

"Both."

I shook my head. "You can't just wander about the boat. There is no way you can explain your presence or have boarded the boat without anyone noticing."

"Then what should we do?"

"Give me a sec." I looked over at Glinda, who held up her hands, indicating she didn't know. I snapped my fingers. "I have an idea."

chapter twelve

"WHAT IS YOUR BIG IDEA?" Genevieve asked.

"I have two theories," I said. "Either Bella seriously upset someone on board in the two days she was alive, or her voodoo priestess grandmother put an evil spell on someone. That person—or their relative—followed Bella to the boat with the intention of killing her—or should I say, succeeded in killing her."

Glinda whistled. "Here, I thought I had crazy ideas."

I chuckled. "I know it sounds outrageous, but there doesn't seem to be any other option. I sent Lorenzo, the vampire ghost, to New Orleans to speak with Bella's grandmother to find out if she'd put a curse on someone connected to the cruise."

"What did she say?" Jaxson asked.

"Lorenzo said that the grandmother admitted to issuing one on Captain Fenton's wife. I don't think he asked why though. My plan is to see if Genevieve and Hugo can follow up with Mrs. Fenton to see what happened—if anything."

Iggy looked up at me. "Do you really believe in curses?"

"Voodoo curses?" He nodded. "I'm not sure, but bad people often do evil things."

Jaxson moved over to his computer. "Let me see if I can find an address for Captain Fenton. Did you say he's from New Orleans?"

"I don't know where he lives, just that he and his wife must have been in town if the grandmother put a curse on Mrs. Fenton. The two of them could have been visiting New Orleans and booked a session with the grandmother for fun, like people do for psychic readings."

"But psychic readings aren't harmful," Glinda said.

"I know that, but maybe they thought Bella's grandmother was a psychic rather than some voodoo priestess."

She nodded.

"I'll look," Jaxson offered. "What's his first name?"

"Michael."

While Jaxson did his thing, I sat on the sofa. I didn't suggest Genevieve or Hugo join me, because they usually preferred to stand.

"I'll get you something to drink," Glinda said.

"Thank you. They don't make ice tea the way you do."

Glinda grinned. "Sweet talking me will get you far."

I tapped my head and smiled. As much as I wanted to watch Jaxson do his magic on the computer, I didn't want to hover.

After ten minutes, he sank back in his chair. "I couldn't find any Michael Fenton in New Orleans."

"That's disappointing. We need to find out where he's from and then what happened to his wife—if anything."

Glinda came out with a tea for me and one for herself and handed me the drink. "Maybe Bella's grandmother put a curse on Mrs. Fenton, but for some reason it didn't work. The priestess might not be aware of that when she spoke with Lorenzo," Glinda said.

"True. That would eliminate the captain from the suspect list if that were the case," I said.

"I have a suggestion," Genevieve said.

"What is it?"

"How about if I pretend to be one of the passengers? I could go up to the captain and say that I think he and I had met before. I could then find out where he lives."

I had to think about that. "That could work. The captain doesn't interact with the passengers very often, so he wouldn't know you aren't one of the fifty-five guests on board. I would know you weren't one of the regulars since I take pictures, but it would never enter his mind that you just teleported onto the boat."

Genevieve clapped her hands and grinned. "What should I wear?"

"Casual attire, but look nice. These are rather wealthy people."

"I know just the thing." She turned to Hugo. What she said telepathically, I don't know, but the two of them disappeared a moment later.

"There goes my way back to the ship," I said.

"They'll be back at some point, but what if someone comes looking for you in the meanwhile?" Glinda asked. "That could cause a stir."

"If that happens, I guess I'll have a lot of explaining to do."

For the next hour, while we waited for our two gargoyle shifters, we all caught up. I hadn't realized how much I missed being with my cousin, her fiancé, and my little iguana buddy.

"Iggy, how is your raccoon friend, Bandit, doing?"

"He's good. I've been keeping him company whenever Genevieve and Hugo are out and about. Bandit has calmed down a lot now that he has two people who pay a lot of attention to him."

"That's really good to hear." Bandit had been quite a handful when he first arrived in Witch's Cove. "And how is your ongoing battle with the seagull, Tippy?" Tippy seemed to have it out for Iggy.

"Since it's high season here, the extra people on the beach are keeping him busy. I saw him the other day, but I hid. I don't think he spotted me."

I inwardly smiled. "That's smart to keep a low profile."

"I wonder when Genevieve is coming back?" Glinda asked, focusing on the immediate issue.

"I hope soon. I have to get back to the ship."

"Knowing her, she might try to find the wife once she learns where the captain lives," Jaxson suggested.

I huffed. "I bet you're right. She is rather headstrong." Genevieve loved to be the hero when it came to solving a case.

"She wants to feel useful," Iggy said.

"I know, but I don't have the sense she understands what is at stake."

I checked my phone for the umpteenth time. Ugh. I'd been gone too long. Because Bella and Lorenzo couldn't solve the crime by themselves, they might be frantic that I was missing. The last thing I needed was for the Coast Guard to be involved in searching for my body at sea.

Thankfully, the wandering duo showed up ten minutes later. "What took you so long?" I shouldn't have sounded angry, but there would be issues if anyone came looking for me.

"We had to do some follow up."

That figures. "Did you find out where the captain and his wife live?" Jaxson asked.

"Yes. He's from Tallahassee, but his wife is dead."

I sucked in a breath. "When did she die? Please tell me it was a long time ago."

Genevieve shook her head. "No. It was a month ago."

"How did she die?" Glinda asked.

"She had a stroke."

"That's terrible, but that doesn't sound like a curse caused it," I said.

"It could have," Glinda said. "You should ask Bella if her grandmother could do something like that."

"I will. I also want to learn more about Bella's job aboard the ship—like whether the captain suggested to Mr. Benoit that she could work for him, or was it the other way around? Bella's dad implied he'd asked."

"Why would that matter?" Genevieve asked.

"If the captain made the suggestion, maybe it was because he wanted to kill Bella."

"Rihanna, you do know that the captain is just a hired hand? It's the owner who might have made the arrangements," Jaxson said.

"That's true, but I thought Mr. Benoit said it was the captain who made the arrangements and not the owner, but I could have misunderstood him. Let me see what Bella knows. If she is clueless, I can contact her father and ask him." The problem was that I hadn't had the time to ask for his contact information. I looked over at Jaxson. "Can you find out the man's phone number? He runs a bank in New Orleans. I figure there can't be that many Benoits who are bankers." Bella would have the information, but Jaxson would be faster.

Jaxson smiled. "Sure." Less than three minutes later, he found the information. "I'll text you the phone number of the bank as well as his email address."

"Great." I turned to Genevieve. "Would you mind escorting me back to the boat now?"

"Sure."

Before I had the chance to hug anyone goodbye, I was in my cabin. I truly believed Genevieve would always act first and think later. Then again, she wasn't totally human.

Bella and Lorenzo were floating about, which I now thought of as ghost pacing.

Bella flew toward me. "What happened to you?"

"Genevieve teleported me back home, because she thought I was in danger."

"Hi, again." Genevieve waved at the ghosts.

Bella got in Genevieve's face. "Why did you take her?"

I would have intervened, but it wasn't as if I could grab Bella's shoulder and restrain her. "Bella, it's okay. My friends were worried. That's all. They want to help."

Bella backed off. "Some help."

"What happened?" I asked.

"The captain wanted to speak with you," she said.

The captain? Since when did the head guy interact with the crew? "What did he want?"

"Hmm. Let me see. Lorenzo, when you and he were chatting, what did he say?"

I held up a hand. "I get it. You guys can't communicate. Sorry. I keep forgetting you aren't alive." Though I wonder how she found out about the captain's request.

"That's okay." Now she sounded rather dejected.

I looked over at Genevieve. "Did you say anything to the captain about knowing me?"

"No! Besides, I was too busy flirting."

"Good to know." I glanced over at Hugo whose lips were pressed tightly together. Clearly, she didn't understand that talking about another man in front of her mate-boyfriend, wasn't smart.

"Nobody knows why he wants to see me?" I asked.

Before anyone could answer, someone knocked on my cabin door. Uh-oh. Instantly, Genevieve and Hugo disappeared. Most likely they'd cloaked themselves. Knowing Genevieve, she'd want to stay around to find out what was going on.

"Answer it," said Genevieve from somewhere in the room.

I pulled open the door, half expecting the captain. Instead, it was April, my immediate boss. "Hey."

"Where have you been? We need to go over the final shooting schedule." She sounded just a tad irritated.

Yes, where have I been? "I'm sorry. I wasn't feeling well."

"I stopped by your room an hour ago, but you weren't here."

"I was in the bathroom." I stood taller, hoping she would stop the inquisition.

"Did you see the doctor?" April sounded a bit more concerned, but I couldn't tell if it was an act or not. People with the ability to close off their minds frustrated me.

And why was she grilling me? I hadn't done anything wrong. Not really. "No. I had a headache, but it's gone. You don't want to know the details. Trust me."

The tension in her shoulders seemed to lessen at hearing a logical explanation. "Glad to hear it."

"What do you need me to take pictures of?" I'd taken several hundred already.

"When the guests disembark the day after tomorrow, we'll have them pose in front of a green screen. I need you to take their picture one more time."

That sounded lame, but I wasn't going to complain. Even though I had a killer to catch, I'd do it. The problem was that I only had a day and a half to find this criminal. "Sure, thing. What time?"

"After lunch. We dock at two."

"Okay."

April, thankfully, turned around and left. I thought it odd that she'd have to tell me about the photo shoot now. She could have waited until tomorrow. Had the captain asked her to spy on me?

I faced the group. "I'm going to see what the captain wanted to speak with me about."

"Wait!" Genevieve said. "The captain could be dangerous."

That was possible since Bella's grandmother put a curse on his wife, and then the poor woman died shortly thereafter. "I doubt he'd stab me in the neck if people are around."

She held up a finger. "Hugo can be your invisible bodyguard. If the captain or anyone tries something, Hugo will incapacitate him."

I was well aware of Hugo's ability to put some kind of paralyzing effect on a person. It didn't last long, nor did it hurt the person, but it would allow me to escape. "I appreciate it."

Not that I knew exactly where the captain would be, but I hoped he'd be driving the boat. "Follow me, Hugo."

Once my gargoyle shifter bodyguard disappeared, I left the room and assumed he was following me. Even if I asked him if he was there, Hugo—being mute—couldn't have answered, though he could have tapped me on my shoulder.

I made my way upstairs and entered the helm. "Excuse me, sir. Someone mentioned you wanted to see me?"

That someone had been Bella. I hoped that wouldn't be a problem. If he asked, I'd say I couldn't remember who had told me.

He spun around. "Yes." Captain Fenton turned to his second in command. "Buck, take the helm. Ms. Samuels and I need to talk in private."

That sounded serious, but I wasn't worried since Hugo would be with me. I liked that I had a bodyguard.

I thought the captain would escort me someplace really private, but instead, he led me to the hallway not far from the helm. I had no idea how many people would pass by, but it seemed safe enough even without Hugo.

"I've heard through my sources that you've been asking about me and my family."

I swear every cell in my body froze, but only for a moment.

My father was an FBI agent, and I was certain I had inherited his ability to keep calm. I couldn't imagine Jaxson's quick search would send up red flags though. I mentally snapped a finger. Genevieve. She never was careful. "Really? Who said that?"

"That's not important, but I can guess why you asked."

This should be good. "Why would I ask about your family?"

Let him answer that one.

chapter thirteen

"BECAUSE YOU ARE TRYING to find out who killed your roommate," Captain Fenton said.

"That part is true, but how—"

He held up a hand. "I was told that someone was asking about my wife. Apparently, you learned that Bella's grandmother was hired to put a curse on Erica, but trust me, it wasn't a curse that killed my wife."

I wondered how he could be so certain. I also wanted to know how he found out about the curse. This case was becoming more and more curious. "Oh. Good to know. So how did your wife die?" I probably shouldn't have asked since it didn't seem to have any bearing on the case, but I wanted to see if Genevieve's intel was accurate.

"My wife had a congenital heart condition and was on medication for it. When she took a turn for the worse, she underwent a procedure that sadly caused her to have a stroke."

I sucked in a breath. "How sad."

"I agree. So you see, it wasn't any voodoo curse that killed her."

"I'm sorry." Though the curse could have been responsible for the procedure failing. If the captain didn't believe it, he wouldn't have killed Bella. Unfortunately, my curiosity wouldn't stop. "May I ask how you learned that a curse had been placed on your wife?" I doubt anyone would have told him.

"Her coworkers leaked it. You see, my wife was a loan officer at a large bank. Cheryl, the woman who worked for Erica, thought she deserved the position more than my wife. It was Cheryl who visited some voodoo high priestess in New Orleans. After some digging, I learned that priestess was none other than Bella's grandmother."

"Oh, my. I'm surprised you let Bella on the boat then."

His lips curled up at the ends briefly. "I am a man of science. I don't believe in voodoo. I let Bella on the ship because her father asked if I could take her. He and his family had been threatened by an irate client, and he thought if Bella were on the cruise that she'd be safe."

Clearly, that hadn't worked out. "Bella said that her father made her get a job. He didn't mention anything about her being in danger."

I didn't think it wise to let him know that I'd spoken with her dad. The captain nodded. "Curtis didn't want to worry his daughter."

"I see. Are you from New Orleans?" I knew he wasn't.

"No, but my wife worked for a bank in Tallahassee that had a branch office there. She would often visit for meetings. And before you ask if she knew Bella's dad, the answer is yes. She met Curtis Benoit at several conferences they attended."

"You met him through your wife, I take it?"

"Actually, we first met when I was asked to take care of the purchase of this boat a few years back. Curtis' bank handled the transaction. And in case you're wondering, my boss paid for the ship, not me."

"Of course."

"Look, Rihanna, if you had any idea that I harmed Bella, you couldn't have been more wrong."

"I can see that now. I imagine you assured Bella's dad that nothing would happen to her and then it did."

"Yes. I was horrified when I found out Bella was murdered under *my* watch."

I didn't have to read his mind to know his pain was real. "I'm sorry for the loss of your wife and for what happened to Bella."

"Thank you." Since he seemed to be in a sharing mood for a change, I had to ask who he suspected. "Do you have any idea who might have killed Bella? Or do you think Matty did it?"

His eyes widened. "You are perceptive. We found a syringe and insulin in Matty's cabin, which was why the over-zealous Mr. Weber arrested him."

I didn't know that. "Maybe Matty is diabetic."

"He is, which is why I'm releasing him. Possession of insulin doesn't make him a killer."

I blew out a breath. "I agree. Any other suspects then?"

His half smile was brief. "That, young lady, is for me to know and for you not to do anything about. We'll be docking in Tampa the day after tomorrow. We'll let the authorities figure it out."

"As soon as we dock, the killer will disappear. I'm guessing you'll have to clean the ship right away, and that any evidence you might have missed the first time will be destroyed."

He pressed his lips together. "Yes, but I have faith in law enforcement."

I didn't. Especially, if any kind of magic was involved. That was slim, but I didn't want to discount it. "What about Mr. Benoit? Friend or no friend, he'll want answers. He's a powerful man. You'll need to do everything you can before you dock."

That seemed to take the air out of his lungs. "You are right. Fine. If you can be discrete, ask around, but don't talk to the passengers. We can't have the press."

I understood that. "I'll be careful."

When he didn't say anything else, or attempt to drag me to my cabin and lock me in, I left. Once back inside my room, the four magical beings surrounded me.

"What did the captain say?" Genevieve asked.

I went through the conversation, sure that if I missed anything, Hugo would fill her in. He had appeared the moment we'd stepped into my room.

"Do you believe him?" Bella asked.

"Actually, I do."

"I still can't believe my dad wanted to protect me." She huffed. "It's so ironic."

"What is?"

"My whole life I've wanted my dad to care about me. The one time he does, and that action gets me killed."

I started to place a hand on her arm for comfort, but then stopped when I realized she was a ghost. "I truly believed he's always loved you, but he just didn't know how to show it. All he wanted was to keep you safe."

"A lot of good that does me now, but I would like to see him one more time."

I waited for her to realize that her dad might not be able to see her. I was about to mention it when I recalled a movie in which a ghost could be seen if the person was emotionally close to the living person, so I chose not to respond.

"Is it true that Matty is really diabetic?" Lorenzo asked.

"I see no reason for the captain to lie. If he didn't believe it, he wouldn't have released him."

"So now what?" Lorenzo asked.

I checked the time. "It's time for dinner. Maybe I can pick up some information in the galley." I took one step and then stopped. "But first, I should call Bella's dad to confirm that he and the former Mrs. Fenton knew each other. One can never be too careful."

"That's a good idea. I wish I could talk to him," Bella said, sounding rather despondent.

"I'm sure he'd really like that. At some point, I could act as a translator if you like. He could ask you questions that only you would know the answer to."

She smiled. "That sounds good, but let's wait until we return to land. We don't want Dad to think you are crazy."

I chuckled. "It won't be the first time." I only had her dad's work number, so I asked Bella for his private line. Once she told me, I called him, hoping that not only the signal was good, but that he'd answer."

"Hello?"

"Mr. Benoit? This is Rihanna Samuels, Bella's roommate on board the ship. We spoke the day you flew to Mexico?" Please remember me. It was possible the man was too distraught to keep names straight.

"Yes. Of course. Did you find out what happened to her?"

"Not yet, but I had a conversation with the captain. I wanted to make sure that what he said was the truth."

"I'm sure it was. Michael is a stand-up guy. His wife and I were friends—as were he and I."

"That's good to know."

"I hope you are focusing your attention on the person Mr. Shephard might have hired."

The possible hit man. "I have no proof, but there is a rather strange man on board by the name of Hackett. Does that name ring a bell?"

"Hackett? Can't say that it does. Why?"

I explained how he was by himself during both tours and that he was rather standoffish when I approached him, which was the opposite of most people on the boat.

"Where is he from?" Bella's dad asked.

"I don't know, but I bet the captain can find out—or the owner of the ship."

"Don't bother them. I'll check it out for you. And Rihanna?"

"Yes."

"Thank you for everything. I wish Bella had taken the time to get to know you. I think the two of you would have gotten along just fine."

I was proud of myself for not laughing. Though in truth, ever since she'd passed, she had been a lot nicer. "Me too."

I disconnected.

"What did my dad say?"

I filled them all in. Too bad I hadn't thought to put the phone on speaker. "It seems as if the captain was telling the truth. He is feeling guilty about Bella's death, so I'm thinking he will help if he can."

"Hugo wants you to find Mr. Hackett and ask him about the lady who died in the car wreck," Genevieve said.

"That's not very practical. I can't just walk up to him and ask how he managed to book a cabin at the last minute."

Bella and Lorenzo paced the space. He stopped and faced me. "Where did you say the lady who died is from?"

"Lara Finley? Russ Tremaine told me she was from Nebraska, but I think Jaxson mentioned the town. It's late, but I'll text him. He should remember."

"Good," Bella said. "It might be important."

I pulled out my phone again to ask him, and to my delight, he texted me back right away. He said that Lara Finley lived in Netwood, Nebraska. I thanked Jaxson and then told the group what he'd said.

"Do we know where Mr. Hackett is from?" she asked.

"No, but it wouldn't prove anything whether he lived in Netwood or not."

"How are you going to get the goods on this guy then?" Bella asked.

"Get the goods?" Lorenzo's brows pinched—kind of. No surprise that he wouldn't know that idiom.

"She wants to know how I can find out about Mr. Hackett," I explained.

Hugo moved over to Genevieve, though why I don't know. It wasn't like he was whispering something in her ear.

"Hugo said he'll find out for you."

"I don't think that's a good idea, Hugo." I wanted to say more, but he was already gone.

"Where did he go?" Lorenzo asked.

I explained how Hugo could extract information from people's minds. "Sometimes."

"Then why not go through each stateroom and do that mind thing with everyone?" Bella asked. "How long could it take? A few hours?"

"I think it's hit and miss with Hugo," Genevieve said. "He's better at making people say things they wouldn't otherwise say. Just reading their minds is more Rhianna's specialty."

"I used to be able to do that." Lorenzo lowered his head. Poor guy.

I held up my hand. "Note that I'm only successful when they don't block me."

I sat on the bed while I waited for Hugo to return. When he did, he took a while to relay the information to Genevieve.

She faced us. "Mr. Hackett was asleep and Hugo didn't want to wake him, but he placed a hand on the man's shoulder. When he did, Hugo sensed a lot of grief pouring off him."

"I felt that too. The man was distant at the pyramid. Pensive almost."

"What does that mean?" Bella asked.

"I'm not sure. Perhaps if I see him tomorrow, I'll ask him why he's so sad," I said.

Genevieve placed a hand on my arm. "Hugo will be with you when you do."

"Thank you. Now, if you all don't mind, I'm starving. Since none of you eat, I'll go by myself, and if I'm lucky, Matty will have been freed and in the galley."

"Since you need your privacy, we'll be in the hallway until morning," Genevieve said.

"That is sweet of you, but talk softly. I can hear you."

She grinned. "We'll try."

Before I reached the door, the four of them disappeared. Even though I had witnessed my gargoyle friends appear and disappear, I don't think I'd ever get used to it.

Once I left my room, I made sure to shuffle my feet until I was down the hallway. I didn't need to trip over Hugo or Genevieve. Being cloaked was quite different from not being there. At least with ghosts, I couldn't feel if I ran into them, other than if I experienced a cold chill.

I headed to the galley. About five people were there, including Matty. I didn't see Haley, which was fine by me.

I slipped in next to him. "I'm glad the captain was smart enough to figure out you were innocent."

"You can say that again. Let me tell you. It was scary. I'd never been in jail before. The weird part was that I kind of liked Bella, even though I'd only just met her. Why would I kill her?"

I nodded. "I know, right? But I guess Mr. Weber spotted the syringe and assumed you were guilty."

"He's a clown."

"I'd keep your opinion to yourself. I wouldn't put it past Mr. Weber to plant evidence in your room just to say he found the killer."

Matty sucked in a breath. "He wouldn't."

"He might."

Matty sipped his coffee. "You're right. I need to keep a low profile. We only have one more day before we dock. I can last that long."

I didn't want to waste the opportunity of asking Matty a few things. "During your detention, were you able to think of anyone who might have wanted Bella dead?"

"No, and trust me I thought long and hard. I know that Chef Goddard was upset that his own daughter was booted off the ship so that Bella would have a place to sleep, but that's all."

I stiffened. "Wait a minute. What do you mean?"

"Tessa Godfrey has been on all of the cruises that I've been on. Her mom passed a few years ago, and she wanted to be with her dad whenever possible. It's why she worked in the kitchen right beside him."

Now I could understand why he disliked Bella so much. But was it enough to kill her? "Can I ask why you came to my room?"

"Sorry about that, but I was worried someone wanted to harm you."

That was consistent with what Hugo found out. "Who?"

"If I knew that, I might be able to figure out who killed Bella. I heard muffled voices in one of the hallways. Your name was mentioned, along with the fact that they needed to take care of you. When I looked to see who was talking, no one was there."

"Was it a man's voice or a woman's?"

He shrugged. "There was noise coming from the rooms. I'm sorry, Rihanna. I couldn't say for sure."

"Thanks for worrying about me."

chapter fourteen

"BACK TO THE chef's daughter. How old is she?" I asked Matty.

He pressed his lips together. "I don't know. Early twenties maybe."

"Did the chef complain to you when Tess lost her spot to Bella?"

"He did. I don't know when he found out about the change, but as soon as I came on board, I asked about Tess. That's when the chef told me about the switch."

"How did the chef sound?"

"Angry. He dislikes rich people being given favors."

I bet no one knew that Bella's family had been threatened and that her dad assumed the boat would be safe for her. "Did he say he wanted to harm Bella?"

"He didn't ever say the word *murder*—at least not in the way you're thinking, but I wouldn't put it past the chef. He is the controlling type."

I leaned closer. "Did the chef know you were diabetic?"

"Sure he did. He makes certain there is food in our kitchen that I can eat."

My mind spun, and not in a good way. Haley came in, and

the look she gave me could have cut steel. If I had been absolutely certain she had nothing to do with Bella's death, I would have told her what the captain said about why Bella was on board.

I quickly finished. "I have to find a few people. Not everyone has been around for me to take their picture." That was lame, but they seemed to buy it. I picked up my dishes and excused myself. Painting on my finest smile, I looked over at Haley. "Hey, Haley. Have a good day."

I rinsed my dishes in the sink and placed them in the dishwasher. I left as quickly and unobtrusively as possible. Knowing that Hugo was by my side helped keep me calm.

I headed back to the cabin to fill the others in on what Matty had told me. Hugo was visible in the room when I stepped in.

"Hugo said the chef might be guilty?" Genevieve said.

He must have told her that when we were still in the galley. I hadn't realized his ability to telepathically communicate was that efficient.

"Yes."

"Tell us," Lorenzo said.

I detailed what Matty told me, including the fact that in order for there to be a bed available for Bella, the chef's daughter had to be replaced.

"We should send some people after the chef and take him down," Lorenzo said.

"What are you talking about?"

"When someone commits a crime against your family, you take justice into your own hands." It almost looked as if Lorenzo threw his shoulders back.

I held up a hand. I didn't need him rushing out of here, though what harm he could do, I don't know. Very little, I suspected. "That might have been the way it was a hundred years ago, but we have laws against that now."

"You mean, I can't do anything?"

Even if I'd said yes, I didn't think he had the ability. "No."

He grunted. "I wish I could bite him in the neck and suck out his blood."

"Eww. Lorenzo. For the remainder of the trip, please refrain from sharing those thoughts," I said. "That would be considered murder, and you'd be just as bad as Bella's killer."

"Fine, but just so you know, vampire bites usually don't kill the victim." He floated across the room and turned to the side.

I couldn't believe he was exhibiting such passive aggressive behavior. I hadn't seen this temperamental side of him before. I turned to Hugo. "I want to see if I can find Mr. Hackett."

"I thought you said my dad was going to gather information on him," Bella said.

"I did. I forgot." I was tempted to see what I could find out myself, but it would be best if I was armed with some knowledge. "I also forgot that Mr. Hackett is sleeping. Speaking of going to bed, I know it's a bit early, but I'm tired. I need to shower and then retire for the night.

Bella went over to Lorenzo. "It's time to go, old man. Rihanna needs her privacy."

How nice. Once everyone left, I cleaned up, changed into my pajamas, and crawled into bed to finish sorting through my pictures. Tomorrow I had to figure out who killed Bella.

Even though I'd set my alarm for seven thirty, I woke up earlier than that. I'd slept amazingly well, which was probably due to the fact that I had four bodyguards watching out for me—though only one or two could actually do anything to save me. I wish I could say that I'd figured out how to learn more about

Mr. Hackett, but I hadn't. And it wasn't as if I could sit next to him at breakfast and start chatting. Besides, I didn't think he ate in the main dining room.

Aha. That was it. Someone had to deliver his meal, right? If I found out who was assigned to his room, I could ask to take in his food tray.

With renewed energy, I cleaned up and then opened my door. "Come on in," I told my sentries.

"Sleep well?" Genevieve said.

"Yes. Any activity in the hallway?" I hadn't heard anything, but maybe I was asleep.

"Nothing," she said.

"I have a plan on how I can find out how Mr. Hackett managed to snag a room at the last minute."

"Do tell," Genevieve said.

"It's not complicated, and it may not work, but I want to try." I told them about delivering Mr. Hackett's breakfast and then asking him about how he was able to book the room at the last minute. I turned to Bella. "How does that work? Does the kitchen staff do room service?"

"The maids handle that sort of thing. I don't think many people eat in their rooms, so it doesn't add a lot of work for them."

"Who would know who was in charge of Mr. Hackett's room?"

"Roberta would definitely know, but I bet she won't tell you. I'd ask Haley."

Roberta was in charge of the maids, and for some reason, she didn't seem to like me all that much. Maybe it was because Bella had been my roommate. While I wasn't looking forward to interacting with Haley, I had spoken with her more than Roberta. "I will ask her." I turned to Hugo. "Coming, big guy?"

He flashed me a smile and then cloaked himself. I began

my search for Haley in the galley, but she wasn't there. Since there weren't too many cabins, I figure I'd eventually find her.

Sure enough, after a few minutes, I spotted her inside one of the rooms. "Psst. Haley."

She looked up and stilled. "Rihanna? What are you doing here?"

I thought telling her that I worked there was a bit too snarky. "I'm trying to find Mr. Hackett's room."

"Why?"

"I want to talk to him. He seems sad."

"So?"

"This is kind of awkward, but I thought I might take his breakfast tray to him if it hasn't been delivered yet. I thought he might want to talk."

Her brows scrunched. "What is this really about?"

Apparently, if I didn't tell her more, she wouldn't give me the information I needed. I told her about the threat on Bella's family. "Okay. Here's the scoop. It's possible, the man who was denied the loan by Bella's dad hired someone to kill her." I made sure to keep my voice soft.

Her eyes widened. "And you think maybe Mr. Hackett is the man who...you know?"

I shrugged. "Maybe." I probably shouldn't tell her about the couple who had reserved the cabin and that the woman died in a car wreck right before Mr. Hackett snagged the room, but I needed her help. So I did.

She sucked in a breath. "Are you thinking he had something to do with that woman's death?"

"I don't know. That's why I want to speak with him. If you were hired to kill someone who was aboard a cruise ship, you'd need a room. What better way to ensure that happening than to orchestrate that person dying?"

"Rihanna, you have a dark mind."

I would consider it more practical than dark. "At times. Do you know if he's had his breakfast?"

"Yes, he's had it, but I don't know if his cabin steward has picked up the tray yet. You can go check. Mr. Hackett is in 3-L."

"Thanks."

"Be careful," she said.

"Not to worry." I certainly wasn't going to reveal that I had my own invisible bodyguard who could incapacitate anyone.

Before she asked any more questions, I left and headed to find Mr. Hackett. What I'd say to him exactly, I didn't know. I hoped something would come to mind.

I knocked on his door, and he answered a few seconds later. "Yes? Oh, it's you."

I wasn't sure what that meant. "I came to pick up your breakfast tray."

"Where is the fellow who delivered it?"

I had no idea. "He's busy and asked if I could get it."

"Fine."

He opened the door to allow me in. When I noticed he'd barely touched the meal, the opening I was looking for jumped out at me. "If you didn't like the food, I can ask the chef to prepare something else for you."

"No, that's very sweet of you, but I'm not hungry."

At the moment, his thoughts cleared, enabling me to see into his mind. "You seem sad." I hoped it wasn't because he'd killed Bella and now felt remorse. No, that was dumb. Hired killers were probably sociopaths.

He stiffened for a moment. "I am."

"I'm sensing a loss." As soon as those words were out of my mouth, I wanted to take them back. He'd wonder how I knew that.

"Did the captain tell you?"

"Tell me what?"

"My sister and her husband had reserved this room for a getaway. A few days before the cruise, she was in a hit-and-run accident and died. I was devastated—still am, in fact. James, her husband, insisted that I go. He thought that my sister would have wanted that."

I wanted to crawl into a hole. All of his actions made sense now. No wonder he wanted to be by himself. He was grieving. "I'm really sorry, but it's a beautiful sentiment."

"Thanks."

I was about to leave when I remembered I'd come in for the tray. I picked it up. Being a gentleman, Mr. Hackett held open the door for me, and I left. I needed to find the person who had been assigned to clean his room so I could tell him not to bother Mr. Hackett.

As luck would have it, I ran into another maid, Rosanna Sanchez, and asked her. She told me who was in charge of Mr. Hackett's room. Just as she was about to question me further, I told her I had a meeting with April that I was already late for. She nodded and went about her business.

Oh, my. The lies were mounting. I found the cabin steward, Sam, and explained that I was chatting with Mr. Hackett when he asked me to take his tray back.

"Thanks for letting me know."

Crisis averted. I returned the tray to the kitchen and then hightailed it back to my cabin. How could I have misjudged the man so much? Waves of self-doubt washed over me. What had I been thinking that I could be some amateur detective? I wasn't my cousin. I was good at taking photos, and I should stick to that profession.

As much as I didn't want to admit it, I felt rather defeated. I climbed onto my bunk and wrapped my arms behind my head.

"What's wrong?" That was Genevieve.

I turned toward her. I hadn't even noticed she was in the room. Hopefully, she'd cloaked herself beforehand. "Where are the others?"

"In the hall."

"Can you ask them to come in? I'll tell all of you about my problem. I need some help."

"Sure." Genevieve left and returned a moment later with the other three.

"What's up?" Bella asked. "I take it Mr. Hackett had some kind of alibi?"

"You could say that." I explained about Lara Finley being Mr. Hackett's sister. Her husband insisted that Lara would want her brother to take the cruise.

"Do you believe him?" Bella asked.

"Yes. His mind was quite open. The man was grieving." I glanced over at Hugo. "Hugo thought so too."

He nodded.

"So now what?" Lorenzo asked.

"Someone killed Bella. Who do we have left who we haven't eliminated? And I'm talking about people who had a reason for wanting Bella dead."

They all looked at each other. When Genevieve stepped forward, I didn't have the heart to tell her that this wasn't some kind of trial where the lawyer needed to step in front of the jury.

"Hugo votes for the chef."

That was my choice too. "Tell me why."

"He has the most motive, because it was Bella's rich father who pulled the strings to have his daughter replace chef Godfrey's daughter."

"Matty said the chef was nice to him in that he made him diabetic food." I held up a hand. "Yes, I know all that implies is that the chef isn't the serial killer type. He had a beef against Bella's dad, and he might have taken it out on her."

"And if he fed Matty diabetic food, he would know that Matty had a syringe and insulin, right?" This came from Lorenzo who'd only just recently learned what insulin was. Go Lorenzo.

"You are correct. While the chef is an excellent candidate, let's continue. Who else?"

"I guess Haley, though April didn't like me either," Bella said.

"Great, but we'll take them one at a time. Let's start with Haley. Why would she want you dead?"

Bella floated over to the end of my bed—a position she really seemed to like. "I already told you. She likes Matty, and she thought I was trying to take him away from her, but you know that was the farthest thing from the truth."

"Actually, when you told Matty to bug off, it was Matty who should want revenge, not Haley," I said.

"I thought you said he was innocent," Genevieve said.

"I did, but maybe I was wrong. I misjudged Mr. Hackett, remember? It could be either Matty or Haley. Think about it. When I was on the top deck taking pictures, I kind of told Matty I wasn't interested, and then Matty breaks into my cabin, which implies he's a little crazy."

"I'm not good at this catch-the-killer thing," Lorenzo said. "I'm confused. Now you think it could have been Matty instead of Haley, or are you thinking it could be someone else?"

"I'm open to anyone being guilty. Don't worry, Lorenzo. You'll catch on. Figuring out who killed Bella is a process. We need to list everyone who had the means, motive, and opportunity to do this. Then we narrow it down. That's what I was trying to do."

"What about April or that strange Mr. Weber?" Genevieve asked.

I dropped back onto the pillow. “We’ll never figure this out, will we?”

“I might have an idea,” Bella said.

The excitement in her voice caught my attention. “Do tell.”

chapter fifteen

"HERE'S MY IDEA," Bella said. "We need to find a way to lure the killer into our room and then nab him."

That was her plan? "There is a small flaw in your thinking. Someone wanted you dead, Bella, not me. Why would someone come in and kill me?"

"Matty said he overhead someone say they wanted to take you out. That means if you tell them that you know who killed me, they will need to shut you up."

At first, that sounded a bit ridiculous, but after considering it for a moment, I decided it had promise. "You're saying I should just walk up to, say, the chef and say that I have evidence that he killed you?"

She shrugged. "Why not?"

Clearly, she had never been involved in solving a crime. "What evidence would I say I have?"

Bella looked over at Lorenzo, though I doubted he had a suggestion.

"I have an idea," Genevieve said.

Thank goodness. "Yes?"

"Of the four of us, I'm the only one who can communicate with other people. Let me tell the chef and the others that you can prove he or she killed Bella, but I won't say what evidence you have."

"He'll want to know," I said.

"It doesn't matter. If he's not guilty, he'll ignore me. If he is the killer, he'll want to find out from you directly what evidence you have."

I had to think about that. We docked tomorrow, and after that it would be too late to catch anyone. "The problem as I see it is that any evidence that was in this room is long gone, and the crew will know that. I don't think anyone fingerprinted the room—or at least I didn't see any black powder. What possible evidence could I have—or say I have?"

Lorenzo appeared to stand taller. "If I was told someone had evidence against me that I'd done something, I would immediately ask them about it."

I blew out a breath. "That may be true, but when they ask me, I'll need to show them something—even if it's fake proof. Just because they ask me about my evidence, it won't prove much."

"I know!" Bella said.

Again? I doubted that, but I needed to hear what everyone thought. "All suggestions are welcome."

"We have Genevieve tell each of our suspects that you have evidence, but she does it late at night." Bella smiled.

"What good will that do?" I was missing something.

"That way, they will sneak into your room and try to kill you before you leave tomorrow, but Hugo, here, will stop him or her."

"Better yet," Lorenzo said, "use a dummy so you aren't hurt. We did that once." He smiled. "We put these mannequins in the casino since we'd been given a tip that some mafia guys were coming. When they broke into our place, they shot up the entire room, but no one died."

"If you were all vampires, you wouldn't have died anyway," I said.

"Agreed, but bullets hurt. The mannequins were destroyed, however, and the damage to the casino was extensive, but we were spared."

I had to put all of this together. "You're saying that we should stuff my bed with pillows and wait for this killer to enter?"

"Yes!" Lorenzo was really into this.

"The staff knows about the security cameras. Would a killer chance being caught?"

No one answered.

"What do we have to lose?" Genevieve asked. "I could run home—figuratively speaking—and find a wig to go with the pile of pillows. If no one shows, no harm, no foul."

Where did she learn those phrases? "Okay. I'm game. Where will I be this whole time?"

"How about you sleep on the bottom bunk? Hugo can sit next to you and keep you cloaked," Genevieve said.

She had thought of everything. "So you are going to speak with some of the crew and tell them what exactly again?"

She glanced off to the side. "For the chef, it's easy. I'll say that Matty told me that the chef sounded really upset because Tessa lost her position on the ship, and that he blames Bella."

"That might be true, but that proves nothing."

She shrugged. "I can make up something else, like you saw him go into the infirmary." I shook my head. "And...and the nurse said that when he left, a syringe and bottle of insulin were missing."

"He'll know that's not true. Instead, maybe tell him that Matty saw him sneak into his cabin and take the insulin. If the chef is innocent, he'll want to tell me how wrong I am."

"Guys, that won't work," Bella said. "If the chef is the killer, he'll just hunt down Matty instead of Rihanna."

This was a total mess. “I need my computer. I want to keep all of this straight.”

I grabbed my laptop and opened up a blank document. For the next hour, we went through the best thing to say to each person. Genevieve would implicate me in each case as the person who had evidence of their wrong doing.

After writing everything down, things became clear as mud. “Wait a minute. I think I know of a way to do this. I have pictures of the crime scene. Maybe you could say the person had dropped something when he or she came in, and it was in the photographs.”

Everyone agreed that might work. We then refined the story Genevieve would tell the chef, Haley, Matty, and April, though hers was the weakest motive of them all.

“I like it,” Genevieve said.

I hissed out a breath. "That won’t work for Matty. He knows there is evidence of him sneaking into my room. If I had something on him, why didn’t I bring it up before?”

Lorenzo paced. He then spun—if that’s the right word—to face us. “Guilt can blind a person. Trust me. I know. I think that if Genevieve just hints that you, Rihanna, have physical evidence against this person, they might try to kill you. I mean, if the person killed once, why not a second time?”

“I suppose. On second thought, Genevieve, how about telling them that I photographed the syringe and sent it to the sheriff on the mainland. That much is true. Say that he was able to enhance the image and get a fingerprint off the syringe.”

“What if the killer was smart and wore gloves?” Genevieve asked.

She was becoming quite the sleuth. “That could be a problem. We should look at the videotape and see if the person was wearing gloves.”

“What are you waiting for?” Bella asked. “Talk to Weber.”

She was right. "Fine. I'll tell him about my plan so that he will be ready when we catch this person." Everyone smiled—even Hugo—though I wasn't so sure why. "No wait. If I'd already sent the evidence to a sheriff in Florida, why kill me? What was done was done."

"Talk to Weber," Genevieve said. "he might have a better idea."

"Fine." I picked up my camera to show him the image of the syringe, which unfortunately, didn't have any visible markings on it and left. I hoped Mr. Weber was in his office since it was fairly late.

I knocked, and blew out a breath when the door opened.

"You again."

I wanted to make a face, but I refrained. "I have a plan to catch Bella's killer, and I need your help." He just stared at me. "I can't do this by myself, and you are the security around here."

When his chest puffed out, I knew I'd caught my fish. "Come in."

On the way to his office, I decided to make a few changes to the plan. I told him that I'd be the one to speak with everyone. After all, Genevieve wasn't supposed to be on the boat. "The plan hinges on the fact that the killer didn't wear gloves or wipe down the syringe. Can you tell from the video if this person was wearing any gloves?"

"How did you know we had a video?"

Oh, no. I couldn't say that some ghost found out. "Um." I channeled my dad, who I was sure always had the answer. "Matty said you had surveillance in the hallway."

Mr. Weber's shoulders relaxed. "I do. I guess it wouldn't hurt to show you. I don't want to be blamed if things go wrong, because you didn't know what you were up against."

I wasn't sure what he meant by that, but I smiled anyway.

He cued up the video and played it. Even though the image was grainy, I nearly shouted. "No gloves."

"True, but the person could have put them on inside your room."

"I would think he'd put them on to enter the room so he wouldn't leave prints on the door handle." I huffed out a breath. "Since we don't have much time, I'm going ahead with the plan. I can spread the word and hope they come after me."

"That's too dangerous."

How nice that he cared, but I had it covered. I explained about putting pillows under the covers, and that I would make something for the head. "I have a wig. In the dark, the person won't be able to tell I'm not real. And I'll hide in the bathroom."

Mr. Weber dragged a hand down his jaw and then shook his head. "I can't let you do that. We won't say you sent the evidence to the cops. In fact, let me spread the word about how you plan to give the evidence to the cops when we dock. I'll make certain the whole staff knows."

Genevieve would be disappointed, but that couldn't be helped. "That's a great idea, but someone is going to want to know why I don't just give you the evidence? You are the ship's security."

He turned back around, stopped, and then faced me. "Because even though I asked for the evidence, you refused. I have no legal authority over you, so it was your right to say no." He hesitated. "Better yet, I'll say I didn't ask for it because I don't have any equipment to process the syringe. No one will question it."

"Good. If asked, you can say you heard I had the photo but you haven't seen it—and that would be true."

Mr. Weber nodded. "We'll go with that, but you need to be careful."

"I will." As I turned to leave, I stopped. "What about the

actual syringe? If there is a fingerprint on it, destroying my photo or killing me won't solve the killer's problem."

Mr. Weber leaned a hip on the corner of his desk. "Good thinking. We'll say that when the staff was loading the body, they accidentally knocked the syringe loose, and when they picked it up, they hadn't used gloves."

"I think people will believe that. The crew wouldn't be trained in crime scene procedure."

"Exactly."

Hmm. This little sting operation might work after all. Of course, Mr. Weber was counting on the gossip chain to be in full force. I was betting he would ask the captain to help too—or at least I hoped he would.

Once back in the room, I faced my eager cohorts. "Change of plans."

No surprise, when I explained that Mr. Weber instead of Genevieve would let it leak that I had an image of a fingerprint, she was disappointed but seemed to understand.

"If you all really want to help, some of you can follow Mr. Weber around to make sure the news spreads to the right people."

That caused a lot of conversation. Since I insisted that Hugo stay with me, the other three did the old divide and conquer thing. They each picked who they would follow. Genevieve chose Matty. Once he found out about the fingerprint, she'd move on to Haley. Lorenzo volunteered to stand by the chef to make sure he knew about the fingerprint, and Bella said she'd follow April around. I just hoped we'd covered all the bases.

"Before we go, check out the bed," Genevieve grinned. "I went back to Witch's Cove and picked up a few things. Glinda helped."

I stepped onto the bottom bunk to check out my bed. I found a woman with the long black hair. When I touched the wig, I felt something solid underneath. I leaned over. "Are you kidding me?"

"Glinda called in a favor from the costume shop across the street. He had a ton of mannequins. This one is on loan."

I looked at the shape of the body, which was very realistic. "I'd think this was me, especially if all of the lights are off." I made a shooing motion with my hands. "What are you waiting for? Go and make sure the line of gossip is flowing."

Hugo held up his hands, palms out, as if to ask what exactly I wanted him to do.

"How about standing guard in the corridor? We don't need someone coming in and seeing the mannequin in the bed and me stretched out below. On second thought, forget that. We should be seen—or rather I should be seen. No one would sneak into my room if I was out and about, right?" Hugo nodded. "And when they do come at me with a syringe, you'll be right here to stop them."

He tapped his chest, which I assumed meant a yes. With my camera in hand, I left the cabin. Since we'd be docking tomorrow, I thought the staff might believe that I'd want to take pictures of them doing what they did best.

My first stop was Matty. Yes, Genevieve was probably there, but that was okay. I had no idea who Mr. Weber would speak to first. It could take him quite a while to conveniently run into each of them.

When I reached the rather cramped laundry area, Matty was folding towels. He looked up. "Hey, there. This is a nice surprise," he said.

I lifted my camera and took a candid. "I couldn't help but capture that smile."

"Go ahead. Take all the pictures you want." He placed the towels on a shelf, and I took a few more pictures.

"Perfect."

Matty dipped his chin. "Guess what I just heard?"

When he grinned, I decided that if he were intent on killing me, he wouldn't be so friendly. If it was about the fingerprint, I had to give Mr. Weber credit for moving so fast. "Do tell."

"Rumor has it you know who killed Bella." He stepped closer. "So who was it?"

Curiosity poured off him, but I couldn't be sure if it was because he'd killed Bella or if he really wanted to know. "I don't know who killed Bella, but I'll tell you this. As soon as we dock, I plan to hand over my photo of the fingerprint to the cops. The image is quite visible on the syringe. They'll be able to tell who it belongs to."

That was so bogus. If I had such evidence, I would have sent it to the cops already, but whatever, as Bella would say. I hoped Matty didn't ask why I hadn't mentioned that before.

"I can't wait to find out."

"You and me both."

chapter sixteen

FOR THE NEXT HOUR, I continued taking pictures of the chef cooking, Haley cleaning, and April organizing. From their actions, they all seemed innocent, though none of them brought up the rumor that I had evidence regarding who killed Bella. Had I misjudged someone? It was definitely possible.

Eventually, the ship quieted down, and since I needed to pack and pretend to be in bed should some killer arrive, I headed back to my room.

Was I hopeful that someone would show up? Not exactly, but I had to try. Hugo appeared as soon as I stepped inside, but then he immediately disappeared. A few seconds later, he and Genevieve returned. It had to be frustrating for Hugo not to be able to communicate with me.

"How did it go?" I asked Genevieve.

"Everyone knows that you have evidence, and that when it is processed, it will point a finger at the guilty party."

I smiled. "Perfect. I guess we just have to wait. I'm going to pack." I looked over at Hugo. "While I doubt I'll get any rest sitting in the bathroom all night, I will know that I'll be safe since you'll be here."

“You will be," Genevieve said. "I’ll find our ghostly friends.”

“Leave them for now. They are just going to sit in the hallway anyway.”

“I have a better idea. Why not station them near the chef's cabin as well as Matty and Haley’s place? I can float over to April’s if you like,” Genevieve suggested.

“Why? So you can warn me if she’s coming?” I asked.

Genevieve looked over at Hugo and nodded. “Sure. Why not? And then I can let Mr. Weber know the sting operation is about to go down.”

I needed to work through this. “So the guilty person leaves their cabin, and then you warn me. As this person walks down the hallway, you tell Mr. Weber that he needs to be on high alert, right?”

“Yes. And before you ask what I’ll tell Mr. Weber about who I am, I plan to say that I’m a friend, and that you asked me to help.”

“I think he’ll buy that,” I said.

“Great. When the person opens the door and goes into your room, should we have Hugo incapacitate him or her?” she asked.

“I hadn’t thought that far ahead, but I don’t think so. The person might say he or she was coming in to see if I was okay —like Matty did before. And we both know I can’t say that Hugo did his death grip on the person because he feared for my life.”

“No.” Genevieve’s eyes widened. “I could flip on the light and take his or her picture.”

I chucked. “I can take the picture, but only after he crawls up to the top bunk and stabs the mannequin in the neck.”

“But it will be dark. Are you sure you don’t want me to turn on the light?”

“No, that would alert the person. I can put on the flash.

The photo won't be a work of art, but it will show the person, hopefully standing on the bottom bunk, with the syringe sticking out of the dummy's neck." I ran through the scenario in my head to make sure I wasn't missing something.

"Okay, when that happens, Hugo will let me know, and I'll teleport to Mr. Weber's cabin and tell him he's needed. He'll then rush over here and capture the person," Genevieve said.

"And if he is slow to arrive, Hugo can delay the person by using his paralyzing grip."

"Perfect. I'll tell Bella and Lorenzo what they should be doing."

Neither of them moved. Not that Genevieve took up much space, but I needed more room to pack. "How about if the two of you give me some room for the next hour? I need to gather my things since I'll be departing tomorrow."

They both nodded and then disappeared. Finally. I had a little time to myself. Since I hadn't brought much with me, packing was easy and fast. Other than some toiletries and a change of clothes for tomorrow, I was done in no time.

Since I wasn't tired, and the staff hadn't retired for the night, I wrote Glinda and told her that I had to take one last set of photos and then wait until everyone disembarked before I could leave. I would text her when I had a better estimate of my departure time. I did not give her any details about the plan for tonight as I was quite sure Genevieve had filled her in when she borrowed the mannequin.

As soon as I sent the message, Glinda wrote back that she, Jaxson, and Iggy would be on the docks when I arrived.

Needless to say, this trip had not turned out as I'd expected. While very different than I'd thought, it certainly wasn't dull, though I was excited to return home and put some routine back in my life. Hopefully, Gavin could get away this weekend for a visit since I missed him terribly.

When eleven o'clock rolled around, I decided it was time to wait in the bathroom with my camera in hand. Had the cabin been any bigger, I could have positioned myself someplace else in the room.

I checked the hallway. Of course, I spotted no one since my cohorts would be invisible. "Hugo, it's time."

With that announcement, I closed the door, and he immediately appeared in front of me, probably to assure me that he was there. Hugo knew the routine. He would remain on the lower bunk in his invisible form waiting for the killer.

I grabbed my computer, my cell phone and camera, and hid in the bathroom. The plan was for either Hugo or Genevieve to float into the bathroom should someone enter my room. With the advance knowledge, I'd know to close my computer, turn off my cell phone, and be ready to take a very important photo.

For sure, this was going to be a really long night.

"Rihanna."

The voice entered my brain, but it failed to compute.

"Rihanna Samuels. Wake up. Someone is in your room."

I wasn't sure if it was the repeated message or the insistence that finally roused me. I opened my eyes and almost asked what was Bella doing there. I thought she was watching someone, and that Genevieve was to wake me up. It didn't matter. One of them needed to warn me.

Being semi awake, I realized that someone was trying to kill me—or rather kill the mannequin. I had already stowed my computer and set it and my phone in the sink since it was drier than the floor, and I had my camera around my neck, ready to go.

I placed my ear to the door, trying to decide when I should take the person's photo. If I went out too soon or too late, I'd lose my chance at any proof. "Who is it?" I whispered.

"I couldn't tell."

"Has this person stabbed me yet?"

One second Bella was there, and the next, she returned. "It's hard to tell."

"You're no help. What is he doing?"

She disappeared and then returned. "Climbing onto the bed to reach you."

That was good enough for me. With the camera set to automatic and the flash exposure on, I eased open the door. I let instinct take over since my mind wasn't fully functioning. I lifted the camera and took the picture, the light from the flash lighting up the whole room.

"No!" The voice was female.

Hugo wouldn't let her escape, so I took the few steps to the door and fumbled with the light switch.

"Let go of me." The voice belonged to Haley. Really? Yes, she was a suspect, but I'd had my money on the chef.

I flipped on the switch. "Haley?"

"It's not what you think."

"What? That you killed Bella and tried to kill me?"

"You don't understand."

No one really understood a killer's motive. If I kept her talking, she might reveal her motive. Genevieve had been told that as soon as anyone entered my room that she was to knock on Mr. Weber's door. Let's hope she could convince him to come down to my cabin. "Explain it to me."

"I swear I don't know why I'm in here."

I'm sure Glinda had heard that line a few times before. "I assume it was to kill me."

"Why would I do that?"

"Because you believe I have evidence that implicates you in Bella's death."

She laughed. "Are you crazy? I might have been a little jealous of Bella, but I certainly didn't kill her."

"Then why stab the mannequin in the bed?"

"What are you talking about?"

Because Hugo wouldn't let her escape, I stepped on the bottom bunk and looked at the poor dummy. The wig hair was parted and a syringe was lying on top of it. I didn't dare touch it, but a quick photo wouldn't hurt.

"Hey! What is happening? Why can't I move?" That shout came from Haley who seemed to be paralyzed. Go Hugo.

I jumped back to the floor. "Don't worry. The effect will wear off shortly."

I wasn't about to explain that an invisible gargoyle shifter was preventing her from moving. Just as I was about to decide what to do, Lorenzo appeared in the room. Oh, boy. Now it was really crowed in here. If I spoke with him, it would really freak Haley out.

"I need to talk with you. It's important," he said.

"Stay here," I told her—as if she had a choice. "I need to find Mr. Weber."

Actually, I wanted to speak with Lorenzo in private. Where Bella was at the moment, I don't know. I opened the door and left, hoping Lorenzo would follow. And he did. "What is it? I'm a little busy here with the killer," I said.

"She didn't do it."

What was he talking about? "I have pictures of her stabbing me—or rather the dummy."

"She was being controlled by the chef."

Lorenzo was making no sense. Before I had the chance to hear him out, Genevieve appeared next to me while Bella floated down the hallway toward us.

By the time the others had gathered, it looked like a regular convention. Of the three of them, Genevieve might be able to explain it to me the best.

"I have Haley inside. Bella saw what happened too. Haley tried to kill my dummy."

Genevieve shook her head. "It's a long story, but Haley is innocent."

Now she, too, was talking nonsense. I lifted my camera and scrolled to the last few pictures I took. "I have proof right here. Plus, she is in the room now."

"You need to watch her," Bella said. "She could be destroying evidence."

I thought it sweet that she was worried. "Hugo will see to it that she doesn't."

"Oh. Well, thank goodness for Hugo, but it was Lorenzo who was the real hero," Bella said.

I wasn't able to follow any of this. "Would one of you please explain what happened. And don't leave anything out."

Genevieve took a step forward. "I'll explain. When I spotted Haley coming toward your room, I found Bella and told her to tell you that you were about to have company."

"And she did," I said.

"Since my sentry job was done, I wanted to touch base with Lorenzo who was keeping watch over the chef."

"I had already concluded that April was zonked out in her bed," Bella said.

"Good to know," I said as I faced Genevieve. "Then what?"

I thought her job was to inform Mr. Weber that the killer was in my room.

"Lorenzo told me that chef Godfrey was making a potion and doing a spell to force Haley to come to him. Once in the kitchen, he gave her the filled syringe and told her what to do."

"What did she say?" I asked.

"She already seemed to be in a trance and didn't say much," Genevieve said.

"Let me tell it," Lorenzo said. Genevieve scrunched up her face and then nodded for him to continue. "Being a resident of New Orleans, I was no stranger to the occult. I'd seen my share of spells and such."

"I'm sure you have." I wanted to rush him along, but I'd worked with Genevieve enough times to know that some people needed to go at their own pace. "Go on. The chef was doing a spell."

"Yes. Haley turned around with the syringe and headed to your room. That's when I suggested Genevieve inform that Weber dude."

Dude? He'd been hanging out with Bella too much. I faced Genevieve. "And did you?"

"Yes, but not until after I had videoed much of what happened, and a little more. I then went to Mr. Weber's room and knocked. I think I woke him."

"It is in the middle of the night." She often forgot that normal people had to sleep.

"I know. I know. I told him I was your friend and that the chef was forcing Haley to do something against her will. I had to show him the video before he believed me."

Wow. "Then what?"

chapter seventeen

"YOU CAN GUESS THE REST," Genevieve said. "Mr. Weber followed me to the kitchen. While the chef wasn't chanting any more, his bowl of herbs and stuff was on the counter—and it didn't contain anything edible."

"Did Weber arrest him?"

"He asked him a lot of questions, that's for sure. Naturally, the chef denied everything, but I'm sure Weber will find some evidence if he looks hard enough."

That was a bit disappointing. Footsteps forced me to glance up. "Well, lookie here. It's Mr. Weber. Finally."

He strode down the hall toward us. "Rihanna, are you okay?"

Didn't I look okay? "Yes, but Haley's not doing so well. She's inside."

Both of my ghost compatriots slipped inside. I'm assuming it was to tell Hugo that Mr. Weber was there. No sooner had I opened the door to go in than Haley rushed out. She stopped short when she almost ran into Mr. Weber.

"Just hold it right there, Haley," Mr. Weber said.

"I swear I don't know how I ended up in Rihanna's room.

I didn't try to kill her. Okay, I did, but I wasn't myself. Someone must have drugged me."

"Let's go someplace private. We don't need the whole crew hearing about this."

I placed a hand on Mr. Weber's arm. "Where is chef Godfrey?"

"Don't you worry about him. He's in a place where he can't escape."

The jail—or whatever they called it on a boat. "What are you going to do about Haley?"

"Haley will come with me, and we'll sort things out. Could both you and your friend send me the photos of both Haley and that video of chef Godfrey?"

I had no problem with that. "Sure. To be clear, do you believe that chef Godfrey put a spell on Haley that made her try to kill me?" I didn't see him believing anything that had to do with the occult.

"At first no, but as I said, I saw the video that your friend took."

Genevieve leaned toward me. "Mr. Weber wasn't totally convinced until the chef confessed to doing the spell."

"He confessed? Just like that?" I asked. "Why didn't Lorenzo tell me?" Ugh.

"It was the darnedest thing," Mr. Weber said.

Lorenzo floated in front of me. "Fine. I did my mojo on him, and he confessed. I knew you wouldn't approve, so I didn't mention it."

I wanted to say that wasn't how we did things in the twenty-first century, but now wasn't the time to tell him that. "I can only imagine. Now what?"

"Haley can't exactly go anywhere, being on a boat and all, so I'll ask her to stay in her cabin until I investigate further. It's not like we have more than one holding cell."

"So is the case closed?" I asked. "You believe chef Goddard killed Bella?"

"I won't know for sure until I have proof. The good news is that I have probable cause to check the chef's cabin for evidence—as well as his kitchen. I'm hoping I find something."

"Doesn't he sound like some big-time cop all of a sudden?" Bella acted as snarky as ever.

"Great." I had to ignore Bella as I pulled up the photos. "What's your email address so I can send these to you? The pictures are on my computer."

Mr. Weber told us. "Thank you, ladies. I couldn't have solved the case without you."

Really? He didn't solve the case at all, but if he needed to take credit, so be it. It wasn't my goal to be the hero. I just wanted to get off this ship alive.

"What do you think will happen to them?" I asked.

Mr. Weber shrugged. "If the chef killed Bella, he'll spend a long time in prison. As for Haley, I don't know. I doubt a lot of people will believe that spells exist, but that's for a jury to decide. I'm just hoping I can find evidence in Godfrey's room."

"Haley is innocent." I hadn't meant to whine, but if she'd been forced to do what she did, Haley should be set free.

"I'm not a judge." Suddenly, his face kind of contorted, and then his eyes turned vacant for a moment. Weber blinked a few times. "What was I saying?"

"Just that you wanted to look into Godfrey's cabin and kitchen to see if you could find any evidence that he killed Bella," I said.

I looked over at Lorenzo. He floated above Weber and smiled.

The security officer shivered. "It's cold. I better get going."

"You do that. Let us know if there is anything else we can do to help you."

"Thanks. I think."

Poor man. As soon as he was out of sight, I faced the group. "In the cabin now. I need to find out what just happened."

I had to open the door, but the others arrived their own way.

"You seem angry," Lorenzo said.

"I would say confused more than anything. No, I'm not really confused. I have this sneaking suspicion that you twisted his mind somehow."

Hugo, I believe, had remained in the cabin making him innocent of any shenanigans. He looked over at Genevieve.

"Hugo says he didn't mess with anyone's mind."

"I figured. It was Lorenzo. Seems our vampire has the ability to not only get the female population to do what he wants, but others too."

Lorenzo held up his wispy hands. "The chef killed Bella. He should pay for that. Forcing that poor young girl to take the fall is horrible. What was I to do? I'm thrilled that I haven't lost that talent."

"You made me stick out my tongue."

Lorenzo smiled. "I won't forget. And that cop person was highly confused. He didn't believe in magic, you know. That's why I had to make him forget."

I had tried to delve into Mr. Weber's mind, but it was like navigating a complex set of highways. "I know. In the end, justice was served, and I guess that is all that matters."

Lorenzo grinned. "I was happy to be of service."

Actually, Lorenzo had been very helpful. "I couldn't have done this without everyone's help, so thank you." I turned to my gargoyle shifters. "If you two want to head back to Witch's Cove, go ahead. I don't think I'll need any more protection."

Genevieve looked over at Hugo and then nodded. "If it's okay with you, we'll sit in the hallway until morning and then head home."

That was so sweet of them. "That would be great." I yawned. "I know I have to be up early tomorrow, so if you all would excuse me, I'm going to climb into bed—or rather Bella's old bed—and try to snag a few hours of sleep."

"I can take the mannequin back to the shop now if you'd like," Genevieve said.

"Let's wait until tomorrow. The Tampa cops might want to take a look at it."

"Okay, but that might put Haley in the crosshairs," Genevieve said. "You know how people who don't believe in magic jump to conclusions."

"She has a point," Bella said.

I didn't usually make snap decisions, but in this case, it seemed like the right thing to do. "Okay, take it away then."

One second it was on my bed, and the next, the mannequin was gone. I figured that Genevieve would return it to the costume shop and then come back here to keep Hugo company.

And that was exactly what she did. I doubted he would, but if Mr. Weber asked about it, I'd say I had no idea what happened. Telling him about teleporting gargoyles might add way too much stress to his already disbelieving mind.

Once everyone cleared the room, I didn't bother changing. After I sent the images to Mr. Weber, I tried to sleep.

I must have managed a few hours since I was jarred awake by the sound of my alarm. I grunted. While I always enjoyed taking pictures, I really wasn't in the mood today.

I halted, my heartrate racing. "Oh, no."

I wasn't sure if Genevieve and Hugo had already returned to Witch's Cove or if they were in the hallway. I opened the door and whispered, "Genevieve are you here?"

When she didn't answer, I stepped back into my room and called her on the phone. "Hello, Rihanna."

"Hey. Can you come back to the ship for a few minutes? When Mr. Weber checks his email messages, he'll see the photos I sent of Haley and the syringe. How will I be able to explain that?" That's assuming Lorenzo had successfully erased the man's memory of what happened in my cabin.

"We'll figure it out. Be right there."

"Thanks."

Sure enough, she showed up a few seconds later. How she could follow a moving boat, I didn't know.

"How can I help?" she asked.

I needed a moment to plan. I only saw one option. "We need to get his phone and delete the two photos I sent him."

"Sure, but what if his phone is password protected?"

"Look at you, Genevieve. You have learned so much." She'd only been in her human side for a little more than a year.

"I haven't learned enough to hack into the phone." She snapped her fingers. "I'll see if Hugo can find out."

She was gone in a flash. Both arrived back seconds later. "Thank you, Hugo. Did Genevieve explain what needs to be done?"

He nodded.

"I'll go with him. Between the two of us, and Hugo extracting the information from Mr. Weber, I can get into his phone and delete the pictures."

Relief washed through me. "You are the best."

It took longer than I thought, but they eventually returned. Genevieve was smiling. "Operation photo removal was a success."

I hugged her. "Thank you both."

"Any time."

They both disappeared, and a huge weight lifted off my shoulders. Since I couldn't remember when I last ate, I headed to the galley. My only chore today was to take one last photo of each person at the screen and then upload them to a cloud service for April to deal with. After that, I would be free—and I couldn't wait.

When I stepped into the galley, most of the crew was there and applauded. I looked behind me to see who they were clapping for.

Haley scooted over. "This is for you, silly. We want to say thank you for finding Bella's killer."

I was a little taken aback, but I sat next to her. Matty stood. "What can I fix you? Some eggs or cereal?"

"I'll have the eggs. Thank you. And some coffee."

He smiled. "You got it."

This was a nice change. "Tell me. Did Mr. Weber find any evidence in chef Godfrey's room or kitchen?"

"He did," Matty said as he poured my coffee. "And guess who was missing two syringes?"

"You?"

"Yup. He didn't take my insulin, but there was a vial missing from the infirmary. Unbeknownst to chef Godfrey, the doctor had installed a camera in the main area. They caught him on video stealing. Where he located the key to the cabinet, they don't know."

"Wow. Did the chef say his motive was because Bella's dad bumped Tess from the roster?"

Matty nodded. "The sad part was that it was Captain Fenton who made that decision—not Mr. Benoit."

"That is so sad." I turned to Haley. "Did Mr. Weber speak with you today?"

"Nope, and I'm not sure why. I guess he believed I was *set up*."

I understood why she didn't say the chef put a spell on her. Her coworkers wouldn't believe her.

The rest of the conversation centered around how I knew

the chef was guilty and why I hadn't emailed the image of the fingerprint to the Tampa cops right away. Naturally, I couldn't tell them about my two ghost friends or my two teleporting gargoyle shifters, so I told a half truth. "I did send it to the cops, but I didn't want anyone onboard to know that."

Matty smiled. "Brilliant."

Once we finished eating, it was time for me to help set up the area where the pictures would be taken, and I couldn't be happier to be finished with this trip.

Once the last passenger disembarked, April came over and thanked me for the great photos and handed me my paycheck. "I hope we can call on you again, Rihanna. You did a great job."

"Thanks." I didn't address her comment about returning. I might not mind another boat, but I had no intention of going on this one.

Once April told me I was free to go, I returned to my cabin to pick up my suitcase and half expected Bella and Lorenzo to be waiting for me in the cabin—only the room was empty.

"Hello?" No one answered. "So that's it? Lorenzo you're going to return to your coffin, and Bella, you'll be crossing over soon?" I thought she wanted me to arrange a time for her and her dad to talk.

Yes, I was talking to myself, but I had closed the door. I checked the bathroom and then the hallway again. Really? We spent a week together and no goodbyes? Sure, it wasn't like we could hug, and no, we couldn't exchange email addresses, but it would have been nice to say something to each other—like good luck in the afterlife.

Whatever. I smiled. That would forever be my Bella

phrase. I picked up my suitcase and headed out. I'd already texted Glinda an hour ago. She, Jaxson, and Iggy should be at the docks by now.

When I stepped off the boat, I spotted them waving, and joy filled me. This was my family, and it was where I belonged.

I rushed down the gangway to solid ground. Once I neared, Iggy practically jumped out of Glinda's arms and into mine. "Hi, big boy."

Jaxson slipped my suitcase from my fingertips. With my free arm, I wrapped it around Glinda. "It is good to be home."

"I can't wait to hear every detail."

Iggy crawled up my arm to my shoulder. "I still think you should have taken me."

I laughed. "Maybe next time, buddy. Maybe next time."

excerpt-better late than staked

Don't forget to sign up for my Cozy Mystery newsletter *to learn about my discounts and upcoming releases. If you prefer to only receive notices regarding my releases, follow me on BookBub.*

Here is a sneak peek of book 2: BETTER LATE THAN STAKED

A cold case, a ghost in need of something to do, and a freshly dead victim of a vampire slaying. Now that's right up my alley.

Hi, I'm Rihanna Samuels, a nineteen-year-old mind reader, from Witch's Cove, Florida. When the ghost of the woman who was killed on a cruise ship last month asks for my help to solve the cold case of a hit-and-run in Nebraska, what could I say?

What anyone would: no! That is until she looked so dejected that I had to find out more about the person she wanted me to help. The case wasn't all that interesting, but hey, I was on spring break, and I thought I could convince my boyfriend to help.

Here's the rub. We didn't just end up with the case we started out to solve. Nope. We found another dead body that I feared was the result of a vampire attack. That's when I knew we needed help from our old friend, Lorenzo Bambini, III. Sure, he's a ghost, too, but I was convinced he was the key to solving our case.

"Psst. Rihanna. I need your help."

I jerked up from looking through my camera photos I'd taken yesterday and blinked. "Bella Benoit? What are you doing here?"

My former cruise ship roommate smiled and floated over to the end of my bed. And by floated, I meant her rather translucent being moved toward me. And yes, she is a ghost—one I hadn't seen in weeks.

"Yup. That's me. I haven't aged a day, have I?" The teenager actually spun around and laughed, a sound that was rather foreign since the last time I'd seen her was to help solve her murder.

"No, you look the same." She even had that voodoo doll in her hand. In fact, she was wearing the same nightwear she had on when she was murdered. "I'm surprised to see you, that's all."

She dipped her head. "You mean because I didn't say goodbye when the cruise was over?"

"Yes. I kind of put my own life in danger to help you, and when we solved your murder, you and Lorenzo left, without so much as a thank you." Wow. I hadn't realized how angry I was about the whole thing.

"I'm sorry. It's just that I really wanted to see if I could connect with my dad."

I doubted a person with no magic could see a ghost, but it was awesome that she wanted to try. "And did you?"

"Kind of. He realized I was there, but he couldn't hear me —at least at first."

"At first?" I asked.

"I kind of cheated. I asked my grandmother to act as an interpreter since she could interact with me."

"Cool." That was what I had offered to do, but it made more sense for her voodoo high priestess grandmother to be the intermediary instead. "With your grandmother present, could your father hear you at least?"

"On and off. And when he could, he cried." She shrugged. "He was quite upset about my death and kept telling me it was his fault for sending me on the cruise."

Why did people always blame themselves for things they had no control over? "I doubt your father understood the dynamics on the boat. If anything, the captain was to blame for making the change in room assignments."

"I guess." She sighed. "But that's water under the bridge as you once told me."

"I did. By the way, where is Lorenzo?" The fellow vampire ghost had been her constant companion.

"I don't know. I saw him once in New Orleans, but he was really distracted. I went to find him again, but he was gone."

"That's too bad." I liked Lorenzo. For being dead, he had a great attitude.

In case anyone was wondering who I am and how I met Bella, my name is Rihanna Samuels. Like Bella, I'm nineteen years old, but that's kind of where the similarities stop.

Thanks to a connection from my college, I landed a six-day photo assignment aboard a fifty-five passenger yacht cruise to Mexico. I was incredibly excited until I met my tattooed and pierced roommate. Bella was a piece of work, but I later learned there were reasons for her bad attitude. The sad part was that she was murdered the next day.

As she mentioned, Bella wouldn't have even been on the boat, except that her dad told her she needed to get a job. In reality, he was trying to keep her from being harmed by some wacky bank client. Too bad he didn't let her in on that secret, not that she could have prevented her death.

Bella was sitting at end of my bed like she used to do on the boat when the door to my room opened, and my cousin, Glinda Goodall, stuck her head in. My bedroom was in the back of her office, and she often stopped in to say hi.

She looked around. "Are you okay? I heard you talking to someone."

I wasn't sure why that would be strange. I could have been video chatting with my boyfriend or speaking with him on the phone. "I'm good. Actually, Bella Benoit just showed up needing my help."

Her brows rose. "Oh?"

Even though Glinda was a witch, she couldn't see or hear Bella, which was rather strange as she often interacted with ghosts. Just my cousin's nine-pound, pink iguana familiar could see and hear her.

Speaking of the little trouble maker, Iggy waddled in. He came over to the bed and looked up. "Is that Bella?" He'd spoken to Bella during one of my video chats with Glinda.

She smiled. "It sure it. It's cool to see you in person, Mr. Iggy. You are so dang cute."

Iggy looked over at me. If he could have planted his claws on his hips, he would have. Being called cute wasn't something he liked. "Whatcha doing here?" he asked her.

"I met a lady in the afterlife who had been murdered, and she asked me to help her figure out who did it since the sheriff in her hometown seems to have dropped the ball. You might remember us talking about her. Her name was Lara Finley."

"The woman who was in the hit and run accident in Nebraska?" he asked.

Wow. I was really impressed that Iggy remembered that. Usually, only things important to him stuck in his brain.

"Yes."

"Does Lara have any idea who ran her off the road?" I didn't remember many details when I'd spoken with Lara's brother. At the time, I was trying to solve Bella's murder.

"No. She thinks she must have hit her head, because she kind of lost her memory for the few days leading up to the accident." Bella leaned forward. "I didn't have the heart to tell her that from the way she looked, she hit more than just her head, because ghosts don't like to know that stuff."

I chuckled. "Good to know."

Since Glinda could only hear my half of the conversation, Iggy quietly told my cousin what Bella said.

"What do you think I can do?" I asked.

"I was hoping you'd investigate," Bella said.

I blew out a breath. "Bella, that is sweet of you to want to help her, but I have classes to attend." Actually, I was on spring break, but I had planned on spending time with my boyfriend, who was also on his break from college. "Besides, I'm not any kind of sleuth. Glinda and Jaxson are."

"Oh." Bella looked over at Glinda and waved. No surprise, Glinda didn't respond. Bella sighed. "How can your cousin help me, if she can't see or hear me?"

"That could be a problem, but remember, I'm just a photographer." So what if I'd helped Glinda solve numerous cases as well as solve Bella's murder? When she started to float away, guilt filled me. "Wait."

Bella turned around and smile. "You changed your mind?"

It stunk that I couldn't read a ghost's thoughts, but I had the sense I'd just been played. "Possibly. Tell me more about what Lara said about the car wreck. She must have seen something."

"Not much. Just that some bright lights had raced up behind her right before the car rammed into her rear bumper and kept pushing her until she went down the embankment and into a tree."

"How horrible. I know the accident happened in Nebraska, but was it on a country road where there wasn't much traffic?"

Bella nodded. "And it was at night."

"Who found her?"

"She doesn't know. She was dead."

"Bella," Glinda said. "Iggy just said that you told Rihanna that this dead woman doesn't know who found her. As a ghost, how long was it before you became aware of what was going on in the world?"

"Rihanna, you and your family always ask such hard questions. Tell her that it was a while. As soon as I realized I was dead, I came back to our cabin, but you would know better. When did I show up?"

I had to think. "Maybe twelve hours after you died?"

"Yikes."

"Rihanna," Glinda said. "Since Gavin is free, maybe the two of you could use this as a vacation together. You know him. Gavin will probably spend most of his break at his mother's morgue anyway. He is focused on his medical career."

She had a point. Gavin wanted to be a doctor more than anything. "I'll ask him, but I'm not all that hopeful he'll say yes."

Bella clapped, but as was the case with ghosts, her hands went right through each other. I couldn't imagine how tough it must be to have lost so much.

"You'll come with me then?" she asked as she returned to the edge of my bed.

"How about if I let you know tomorrow?" I needed time to think about it. "If I do go, it will cost money since I'll need a plane ticket and a place to stay. You'll have to understand that I can't be there for more than this week as I have school."

Bella smiled. "That's okay. I told Lara that I'd convince you to help. I don't think she expects you to be successful."

That wasn't very encouraging. "Nice to know." I placed the camera I had been holding on the bed. "If you were with your dad in New Orleans, how did you run into Lara? And how did you even know who she was?" I was quite sure they hadn't met when they were alive.

Bella laughed. "It's not like you die in Nebraska and then float above it for the rest of your life."

That made sense. "Does this mean you've crossed over?"

She tucked in her chin. "No! I'm not eager to find out what's in store for me. Knowing my life, I'd be sent to a place I don't want to go."

I didn't think those into voodoo believed in the conventional Heaven and Hell, but what did I know? "Okay, but how did Lara find you? Was she aware that you were on the same cruise ship as her brother?"

Bella lifted off my bed and floated around—her version of pacing. "I think I was complaining that I had been murdered, and Lara overheard me. I can be a little loud, you know."

I swallowed a laugh. "I do know that. Then what happened?"

"I recognized her name."

I probably would never understand how these two met, but I supposed it didn't matter. "You told her you'd help by asking me to take the case, right?"

"Yes."

It had been quite the adventure trying to find Bella's killer. "I see. Stop by tomorrow, and I'll let you know."

"Okay." As quickly as she arrived, Bella left.

I blew out a breath. “What do you think?” I asked Glinda.

Thankfully, Iggy had translated everything to her. “You should do it,” Iggy said.

I was speaking to my cousin. “Thank you, Iggy. Glinda, any words of advice?”

“I trust you, but you know that you can always ask our two gargoyle shifters to help,” she said.

Genevieve and Hugo could teleport anywhere in seconds. Hugo, in particular, had many abilities to stop a person from harming me should the situation arise. “I know, and I appreciate that.” I slipped off the bed. “I need to discuss this with Gavin. I know he was anxious to learn what he could from his mom during his short break. He might not want to spend time away from the morgue.”

Glinda nodded. “I understand, but if anyone can convince him, it's you.”

“I hope so.”

I thought about calling him, but Gavin might be in the middle of an autopsy. Besides, asking him in person would be better. I grabbed a light sweater and left the office that was situated above Jaxson’s brother’s wine and cheese shop. The wind whipped off the ocean, scenting the air with a deliciously salty bouquet. From the frequent temperature changes we’d been experiencing during the day, spring would be here before I knew it, and with it very warm weather.

The walk to the morgue would take less than ten minutes, which would give me time to decide if I even wanted to help Bella—or rather Lara Finley—a woman I’d never met.

I loved nothing more than taking photos. The creative process soothed my soul, but trying to figure people out and helping others might be an even bigger high.

At the moment, I wasn’t planning on following in Glinda’s footsteps, but seeking the truth was in my blood. My dad had been an undercover FBI agent, and part of what he did appealed to me. Right now, though, I needed to see if Gavin would go with me. I certainly couldn't count on Bella doing much, other than spying on people, and I didn't like asking Genevieve and Hugo to be there on the off chance I needed saving. That wasn't my style.

When I arrived at the morgue, I stepped inside. Since it wasn't a place that people visited, there wasn't a receptionist. I knocked on the morgue door in the hopes Gavin was inside.

A voice came over the speaker. "May I help you?"

"Hey, Elissa. It's me, Rihanna. I'm looking for Gavin."

"He's here. I'll send him out."

"Thanks."

It would take him a while to wash up before coming out. While I waited, I braced myself for all of his objections. Not only would Gavin say it wasn't safe to hunt down a killer—and he'd be right—but he'd correctly note that he couldn't help if he couldn't see or hear a ghost.

Ugh. Solve both of those issues, and we might be on a plane to Nebraska tomorrow.

Check out BETTER LATE THAN STAKED on Amazon.

THE END

about the author

Love it HOT and STEAMY? Sign up for my newsletter and receive MONTANA DESIRE for FREE. Click here

OR Are you a fan of quirky PARANORMAL COZY MYSTERIES? Sign up for this newsletter. Click Here

Not only do I love to read, write, and dream, I'm an extrovert. I enjoy being around people and am always trying to understand what makes them tick. Not only must my romance books have a happily ever after, I need characters I can relate to. My men are wonderful, dynamic, smart, strong, and the best lovers in the world (of course).

My Paranormal Cozy Mysteries are where I let my imagination run wild with witches and a talking pink iguana who believes he's a real sleuth.

I believe I am the luckiest woman. I do what I love and I have a wonderful, supportive husband, who happens to be hot!

Fun facts about me

(1) I'm a math nerd who loves spreadsheets. Give me numbers and I'll find a pattern.

(2) I live on a Costa Rica beach!

(3) I also like to exercise. Yes, I know I'm odd.

I love hearing from readers either on FB or via email (hint, hint).

Social Media Sites

Website: www.velladay.com
FB: www.facebook.com/vella.day.90
Twitter: velladay4
Gmail: velladayauthor@gmail.com

also by vella day

A VOODOO AND VAMPIRE MYSTERY

Call Me Ghostly (book 1)

Better Late Than Staked (book 2)

A WITCH'S COVE MYSTERY (Paranormal Cozy Mystery)

PINK Is The New Black (book 1)

A PINK Potion Gone Wrong (book 2)

The Mystery of the PINK Aura (book 3)

Box Set (books 1-3)

Sleuthing In The PINK (book 4)

Not in The PINK (book 5)

Gone in the PINK of an Eye (book 6)

Box Set (books 4-6)

The PINK Pumpkin Party (book 7)

Mistletoe with a PINK Bow (book 8)

The Magical PINK Pendant (book 9)

The Poisoned PINK Punch (book 10)

PINK Smoke and Mirrors (book 11)

Broomsticks and PINK Gumdrops (book 12)

Knotted Up In PINK Yarn (book 13)

Ghosts and PINK Candles (book 14)

Pilfered PINK Pearls (book 15)

The Case of the Stolen PINK Tombstone (book 16)

The PINK Christmas Cookie Caper (book 17)

Pink Moon Rising (book 18)

SILVER LAKE SERIES (3 OF THEM)

(1). **<u>HIDDEN REALMS OF SILVER LAKE</u>** (Paranormal Romance)

Awakened By Flames (book 1)

Seduced By Flames (book 2)

Kissed By Flames (book 3)

Destiny In Flames (book 4)

Box Set (books 1-4)

Passionate Flames (book 5)

Ignited By Flames (book 6)

Touched By Flames (book 7)

Box Set (books 5-7)

Bound By Flames (book 8)

Fueled By Flames (book 9)

Scorched By Flames (book 10)

(2). **<u>FOUR SISTERS OF FATE: HIDDEN REALMS OF SILVER LAKE</u>** (Paranormal Romance)

Poppy (book 1)

Primrose (book 2)

Acacia (book 3)

Magnolia (book 4)

Box Set (books 1-4)

Jace (book 5)

Tanner (book 6)

(3). **WERES AND WITCHES OF SILVER LAKE** (Paranormal Romance)

A Magical Shift (book 1)

Catching Her Bear (book 2)

Surge of Magic (book 3)

The Bear's Forbidden Wolf (book 4)

Her Reluctant Bear (book 5)

Freeing His Tiger (book 6)

Protecting His Wolf (book 7)

Waking His Bear (book 8)

Melting Her Wolf's Heart (book 9)

Her Wolf's Guarded Heart (book 10)

His Rogue Bear (book 11)

Box Set (books 1-4)

Box Set (books 5-8)

Reawakening Their Bears (book 12)

OTHER PARANORMAL SERIES

PACK WARS (Paranormal Romance)

Training Their Mate (book 1)

Claiming Their Mate (book 2)

Rescuing Their Virgin Mate (book 3)

Box Set (books 1-3)

Loving Their Vixen Mate (book 4)

Fighting For Their Mate (book 5)

Enticing Their Mate (book 6)

Box Set (books 1-4)

Complete Box Set (books 1-6)

HIDDEN HILLS SHIFTERS (Paranormal Romance)

An Unexpected Diversion (book 1)

Bare Instincts (book 2)

Shifting Destinies (book 3)

Embracing Fate (book 4)

Promises Unbroken (book 5)

Bare 'N Dirty (book 6)

Hidden Hills Shifters Complete Box Set (books 1-6)

CONTEMPORARY SERIES

MONTANA PROMISES (Full length contemporary Romance)

Promises of Mercy (book 1)

Foundations For Three (book 2)

Montana Fire (book 3)

Montana Promises Box Set (books 1-3)

Hart To Hart (Book 4)

Burning Seduction (Book 5)

Montana Promises Complete Box Set (books 1-5)

ROCK HARD, MONTANA (contemporary romance novellas)

Montana Desire (book 1)

Awakening Passions (book 2)

PLEDGED TO PROTECT (contemporary romantic suspense)

From Panic To Passion (book 1)

From Danger To Desire (book 2)

From Terror To Temptation (book 3)

Pledged To Protect Box Set (books 1-3)

<u>BURIED SERIES</u> (contemporary romantic suspense)

Buried Alive (book 1)

Buried Secrets (book 2)

Buried Deep (book 3)

The Buried Series Complete Box Set (books 1-3)

<u>A NASH MYSTERY</u> (Contemporary Romance)

Sidearms and Silk(book 1)

Black Ops and Lingerie(book 2)

A Nash Mystery Box Set (books 1-2)

STARTER SETS (Romance)

<u>Contemporary</u>

<u>Paranormal</u>

www.ingramcontent.com/pod-product-compliance
Lightning Source LLC
LaVergne TN
LVHW090947080826
845145LV00003B/924

* 9 7 8 1 9 5 1 4 3 0 4 9 8 *